Boreal

Ingela Karlsson

Boreal

Vanguard Press

VANGUARD PAPERBACK

© Copyright 2024
Ingela Karlsson

The right of Ingela Karlsson to be identified as author of
this work has been asserted by her in accordance with the
Copyright, Designs and Patents Act 1988.

All Rights Reserved

No reproduction, copy or transmission of this publication
may be made without written permission.
No paragraph of this publication may be reproduced,
copied or transmitted save with the written permission of the
publisher, or in accordance with the provisions
of the Copyright Act 1956 (as amended).

Any person who commits any unauthorised act in relation to
this publication may be liable to criminal
prosecution and civil claims for damages.

A CIP catalogue record for this title is
available from the British Library.

ISBN 978 1 80016 882 4

This is a work of fiction. Names, characters, businesses, places, events and
incidents are either the product of the author's imagination or used in a
fictitious manner. Any resemblance to actual persons, living or dead, or
actual events is purely coincidental.

Vanguard Press is an imprint of
Pegasus Elliot Mackenzie Publishers Ltd.
www.pegasuspublishers.com

First Published in 2024

Vanguard Press
Sheraton House Castle Park
Cambridge England

Printed & Bound in Great Britain

To my parents

BOREAL

In Boreal it was always winter and dark most of the time. The barren, open landscape shifted into sky high mountains and didn't invite unnecessary travels through the land. To leave your home unprepared could be very dangerous. Snow, wind and ice could easily catch you and you'd never find your way back home again. Wild animals lurked in the bushes and if you were unlucky you could be their lunch or dinner.

Despite the cold and the dark, terrible accidents hardly ever happened. The Queen of Boreal was a fair and respectful leader whom the inhabitants had great trust in.

On a cold winter's day, the Queen's fastest peregrines carried a message to the inhabitants of Boreal. They flew with the speed of the wind over snowclad mountains, dived down on snow-covered roofs, hidden caves and holes. Their loud *"Ke-ke-ke"* told the inhabitants to leave for the castle at once.

To visit the castle was something that the inhabitants only could dream of. Therefore they left everything that they had at hand and were off in an instant.

The castle, which was surrounded by a moat, rose like a rectangular iceberg in the middle of the frosty landscape. Its towers and pinnacles competed to reach the dark, starry sky. Lots of small fires cast their shadows on its glimmering facades.

The Queen of Boreal was in the right wing of the castle. She wore a deep-blue, long satin dress that had long, wide arms edged with sapphires. Her thick black plait adorned with the beautiful feathers of an eagle formed itself like a snake from the neck onto the shoulder and down to the waist. Her crown, made of the shiniest silver, was placed on a satin-clad stool beside the round table.

Her icy blue eyes searched the gathered: the Powerful, the Ethereal and the Illustrious. There was an edge to her voice as she said:

"As you probably understand, the situation is deeply worrying. I will get straight to the point. It has been three days since I received the message that humans have lost their imagination. The children are born without imagination in their souls and the stories are disappearing."

The gathered froze.

"How is this possible?" the Ethereal asked in a hissing voice.

"I do not know but I have my suspicions," the Queen said worriedly. "A while ago there were reports of one or two humans beginning to lose their imagination and in turn, the stories. At the time it was not very disturbing. But now the situation is totally different. It has gone as far as no human babies being born with imagination in their souls any more. And among the elderly there are few who still can use their imagination and pass on the stories." She went quiet and plucked her plait.

"But why have we not been informed about this earlier?" said the Illustrious. "How could this have happened without our knowledge?"

Its claws made deep cuts in the table. The Powerful quickly put one of its trembling branches over its big paws.

"I understand that this feels like ice in your veins," said the Queen. "We know that this happens every now and again and it has not hurt us or them. But now…" She took a deep breath.

"But why have we not been informed about this earlier?" roared the Illustrious. Its growling jaws made them tremble.

The Powerful rose, waved its knotty tree arms and said, "I have to agree with the Illustrious. Why has this not come to our knowledge until now?"

The Queen snapped her fingers. Two guards entered with a big crystal ball which they placed in the middle of the table. Everyone's eyes turned towards it. The Powerful sat down again.

Inside the crystal ball were sculptures of dim frost which slowly changed shape. The Queen held her hands around the crystal ball and a faint light showed. When she removed her hands the sculptures turned into the shape of a face. A strong cold swept through the room. Sharp icicles formed in the ceiling and icy shivers ran hither and thither across the table. A scornful and distorted face stared at them from inside the crystal ball. Its toothless mouth let out a black, mean peal of laughter which made the icicles loosen from the ceiling and shoot down onto the table like missiles.

Fear struck the gathered and they shivered, not only from the cold. The guards hurried to them with fur rugs which even the Illustrious with its thick fur, gratefully accepted. Suddenly a howling came from the face inside the ball. Mylingar riding on ravens flew out of the mouth of the grotesque face and tried to break through the glass. They banged, screamed and shouted.

"We understand! We understand!" exclaimed the Powerful. "Can you turn it off in some way?"

The Queen swept her hand over the crystal ball. The mylingar dissolved, and the sculptures returned into their form. The strong cold and the icicles disappeared. The Illustrious put its big paws on the table and rose.

"Elakka! It is her. Elakka! She is alive. She is back. It is she who destroys the imagination."

The Illustrious came down on its feet. Its claws made deep cuts in the floor as it growling circled around the table.

"It cannot be possible. Not Elakka!"

The Powerful leaned over towards the Queen and stared at her with burning eyes.

"It can't be true. I thought she would be dead by now or at least locked up and chained forever."

A sputtering spitting sound came from the Etheral's chair.

"And she has a whole army of mylingar to aid her," it hissed furiously. A faint nasty-smelling puff of air appeared when the Ethereal rose from the table. The Powerful held its nose.

The Queen raised her hands.

"My friends," she said in an attempt to calm them down. "Our lives are at stake but we cannot let our emotions take over. We must contain ourselves."

She cupped her hands around the crystal ball and the sculptures gave way to a seldom seen heavenly spectacle. The star constellation of the Lynx showed itself together with Aurora Borealis, the magical Northern Lights. Everybody around the table was caught by the mesmerising scene and they all felt a trifle calmer.

The Queen continued: "It is tonight that the Lynx and Aurora will be seen in the vault of heaven. A sign that we can get unexpected help. But we have a difficult and dangerous task in front of us. We will need all the strength we can muster to destroy Elakka. So tonight I have invited all the inhabitants of Boreal to the castle. They are already on their way but they do not know that their lives are in danger. Time is short and we must begin the preparations."

Sira

Sira sat by her desk in her room and tried to paint. The colours didn't mix the way she wanted and the black bristles on the paintbrush fell down on the paper one by one. She put the paintbrush away and sighed.

The dark outside the window reminded her of how lonely she was. Her mother was at work as usual. She was never home nowadays. Sira flipped through some of her drawings in the sketchbook. If she was at her grandmother's instead, she would have her mouth full of newly baked buns and homemade strawberry juice. Her grandmother would ask how her day had been and she would have told her everything. About Moa, how mean she was at every break. And about the art teacher who went on about perspectives and other boring things. When the juice and the buns were finished she would huddle herself in the blue couch in the living room and her grandmother would sit herself comfortably in her armchair with the crocheted star on the back. And with her round glasses on her nose she would begin to tell an exciting story from the past.

Sira always got such good ideas from her grandmother's stories, which she painted afterwards. It was her grandmother who had taught her to paint, not the art teacher at school. He was just like her mother. In her eyes everything had to be perfect and realistic.

'You have such an imagination, Sira,' she always used to say when Sira turned a toilet paper roll into a spaceship. Or: 'That was nice but I don't understand your weird drawings. Don't you learn how to draw properly at school like using perspectives?'

Her mother's comments smashed Sira's imagination into pieces and it had been like that since she was little. And even more since her parents got divorced because then her mother had to have two jobs so they could stay in the house. She never had any time for Sira. Never ever…

Teardrops bounced on the paper in front of her. No, she refused to be alone for one more second. She dried her face with her sleeve and got up from the desk, fetched her brown rucksack and began to pack her sketchbook, colours, paintbrushes and a warm sweater. Her mother had herself to blame. It was better at grandmother's.

She looked at the watch. Her mother could be home any time now. And she would try to stop Sira and say: 'To your grandmother now? No, you can't. It's school tomorrow.'

Sira hurried to put on her jacket and shoes. The front door slammed behind her and she flew down the stairs. The dark lay like a mist in the garden. She turned on the light on her mobile as she ran as fast as she could over the courtyard, crossed the road and into the woods. She knew that it would grow darker and darker but taking the shortcut through the woods was the fastest way to her grandmother's. She would make it.

The treetops howled and the wind pushed her in between the tree trunks. She tripped. Got herself on her feet again, tripped again; the mobile fell out of her hand and disappeared. She tried to find it but the darkness hid it. Tears formed in her eyes. *I will find the way anyway,* she thought and continued.

The ground beneath her thin white Converses was swampy: damp leaves, needles and moss all over the place. The damp sank into her shoes and her jeans stuck to her legs.

Her pace slowed. She fought to get further into the woods. The tree trunks blocked her way. She bent her head down, forced away twigs and branches which scratched and tore her quilted down jacket. The new one. Tree trunks creaked. A howling scream passed her closely followed by another scream and yet another. She felt something flitting brushing past her, scratching her face.

Something snatched the bobble of her cap. She tried to hold on to it but something pulled and tore it. Something that screamed and howled. Fear crept inside Sira. Who tore her cap? She must get away from here. She must get to her grandmother's house. Now.

A branch hooked into the holes in her jeans, stopping her. She was forced to let go of the cap. It was torn from her head. Bony hands grabbed her hair. Sira screamed and started to run even faster but the bony hands and the howling sounds came after her. She looked desperately around her. Where would she go? She didn't know where she was or where she could hide. What if she couldn't hide? What if it saw her wherever she was…

"Help me!" she shouted.

At the same moment she felt claws gripping her shoulders. Roots climbed fast out of the ground and tripped her up. She fell towards a stone. Her left shoulder gave a twinge when her head met the hard surface of the stone and she fainted.

The gnomes

When Sira regained consciousness she didn't know where she was. She felt the scent of forest and spruce twigs. She turned her head. Ouch! She felt a big bump on her head. Her body was sore and her shoulder ached. A bit further away she saw a flickering light. She groped around with her hands and felt a soft skin rug over her and a bed of spruce twigs beneath her. Besides that it felt as if the ground was covered with leaves. Was she in a kind of hut? Her echoing thoughts were the only things heard inside the little space. *Where am I? How did I get here?* She tried to remember. *What really happened?* She closed her eyes. Her thoughts didn't want to cooperate and her head hurt. At the same time she heard a rustling sound. A chattering of voices followed.

"Have you heard? Have you heard?" a bright voice said. "The Queen has invited everyone to the castle and I mean *everyone*! There will be a grand dinner. There will be a party!"

A hawking was heard and someone with a darker voice spoke: "Have you been to the castle again?"

"We saw that they were setting the tables in the big dining hall. Can you imagine the big dining hall!" the little voice said again.

"And with the best service and everything," another little voice added.

"And the glasses. Did you see the glasses? My, my! How elegant. When I sneaked past the kitchen I heard that they would serve ancient water."

"Ancient water! Can you imagine?" said the dark voice with a sigh.

"And that's not all," the little voice continued. "With cranberries in it."

"Oh, I haven't tasted cranberries in years."

Someone clicked its tongue.

"It has to be something very special going on," the dark voice said curiously. "What if she is getting married?"

"Getting married? I don't think so. There hasn't been any consort here for eternity's eternity."

"That might be so. But there is one that I can think of."

The voice made the others think and it became quiet for a moment before a little voice shouted:

"Who is it? Say, say! I'm dying of curiosity."

"Justice." The little voice sounded decisive.

"Justice? Who is that?" shouted several in one voice.

"I don't know but once I heard the Queen talking to herself and she said that the only passion she had was Justice. Passion means that you're in love with someone, doesn't it?"

"It does for certain. Love and passion belong together I have read," answered the dark voice.

"You're always so wise." The little voice was full of admiration.

"That must be it. The Queen is marrying Justice and that's why she's throwing a party for everybody," said the dark voice.

"This will be so exciting!" exclaimed one of the small voices.

The chattering voices disappeared.

Sira frowned. A castle? A Queen? A party? What was all this?

Another sound was heard. It sounded like something was being pushed through the leaves on the floor. She peered to try to see what it was but the dim light of the little flame wasn't much help. She decided to find it out in another way.

"Hello," she called quietly. "Is there anyone there?" The rustling sound stopped suddenly. Sira waited for an answer but none came.

"Hello," she tried again.

The shape of what she thought was a mug was pushed to her. It smelled nice. And she felt how thirsty she was and grabbed for the mug. She took a large gulp. The lukewarm drink had a taste of resin and something else she couldn't put her finger on. It warmed her insides and the thirst disappeared for a while.

"Who are you and why are you running around in the woods all by yourself?" a little voice said.

Sira jumped and almost spilled out what was left in the mug. The flame grew stronger and stronger and she spotted a small figure among the leaves. Was it a frog? Now she saw another figure and then one more... or was it mice? She shivered.

"We want to know. Who are you and what has brought you here?" one of the figures said.

Sira didn't know what to think or say. Mice that talked? She must have hit her head badly.

"Eehh... My name is Sira and..."

In that moment, the figures transformed into a group of grey clad characters peeking at her with their small peppercorn eyes.

"Sira," one of them said with a bright voice. "You are lucky we saved you, Sira. It really was at the last minute."

"Saved me from what? And who are you?" Sira put her hand on her head. The bump still hurt.

The round faces underneath the woollen caps turned to each other. The character with the biggest snub nose said:

"We are gnomes. What are you doing all alone in the dark forest? You should know that it was very close. The mylingar almost got hold of you."

"You should know that it was very close that mylingar got hold of you," Another gnome filled in.

"You should know that it was very, very close that mylingar got hold of you," said the gnome with the smallest snub nose.

"Enough!" said the gnome with the biggest snub nose irritably. He turned to Sira. "It was we who tripped you up so that you fell."

"If we hadn't done that... Yes, I don't even want to think about what could have happened."

"Mylingar?" Sira said. "Who are they?"

She felt the fear creeping inside of her. She had heard of gnomes but mylingar, what were they?

"Mylingar are horrible creatures and they ride on ravens. Not the ravens you know, these are much worse. They are always awake at night and fly around looking for prey. It was one of them which grabbed you with its frightful claws, so it was good that you asked for help and fortunate that we were in time to trip you up. To lie stretched out is the only way to get rid of them. But we do apologise for you hitting your head on the stone."

Sira felt her bump again. "Yes, it really hurts actually."

The gnome suddenly looked worried.

"Oh dear dearest!" exclaimed another gnome. "Time to hurry up. We have to get ready for the big celebration at the castle. We mustn't be late for the Queen." The gnome urged the others on who quickly pushed off through the rustling leaves. Then it turned to Sira and added, "You're coming as well."

"Me? I can't. I have to get back to my grandmother. She and my mum must wonder—"

"You are coming." The gnome repeated and peeked at her with cunning peppercorn eyes before he disappeared amongst the leaves. Sira closed her eyes. This must be a dream. A perfectly normal dream.

Sira meets Interpreter

The spruce twigs' needles stung her. She squirmed and opened her eyes. It was no dream. She reached out for the mug.

A hawking was heard. She looked around. The flame was stronger now but wherever she turned her head she couldn't see anyone. She sat up. Her head felt better which was nice. She took a sip of the resin-like drink.

"Hrm, hrm."

"Hrm, hrm." " Sira imitated. After meeting with the harmless gnomes she didn't feel afraid of whatever this someone could be.

A figure came into the light of the flame. She had heard about gnomes but she couldn't place this character in any of the stories her beloved grandmother had told her. The character in front of her was short, dressed in a uniform and a smart-looking fur cap.

"Hrm, hrm."

The character looked at her closely with its thin leather brown eyes, brushed off some ice crystals from the right shoulder of its well-ironed uniform and said: "Allow me to introduce myself." He bowed lightly. "My name is Interpreter. I am the Queen's interpreter, multicultural and of the highest rank."

His fur-clad hand stroked the medal on its chest where *For the best translation ever* was engraved with ornate letters.

"As far as I am concerned, there is no better interpreter than myself," the character continued.

"And you are lucky because I was supposed to be at a much finer mission right now. But the Queen insisted."

He sighed deeply.

"Sira is my name," Sira said and looked at the little character. Even if she didn't know his kind, he really looked like a genuine fairy-tale character. "I can't be here right now. My grandmother waits for me and my mother…"

"I know and I am here to get you. Now then, here are your clothes. Hurry up. I'll wait for you in the tunnel over there."

Interpreter gave her a parcel and disappeared before Sira had a chance to say anything.

While Sira opened the parcel she thought about how irritated the uniform-clad figure would be if he knew she thought of him as a figure. She giggled. He would clear his throat and put on airs. The small eyes would be even smaller and the thin drawn-out mouth would purse its lips. Sira almost burst out laughing when she thought about his fur-clad cap being on one side.

The clothes inside the parcel were almost the same as the ones she already wore. The only difference was the shoes. Instead of the white Converse, which were ruined, there were a pair of lined winter boots. And instead of the torn quilted down jacket there was a fur coat. She was happy to get new, dry clothes but still she couldn't understand where she was or why she was there.

"Come now come! We must hurry!" Interpreter's voice echoed from the tunnel.

"I'm coming!" Sira shouted while she buttoned the fur coat. It was nice and warm. Quickly she put on her boots and went into the tunnel.

A stuffy, musty smell reached her nose and she coughed. The tunnel was almost dark except for some small light-filled dots jumping up and down along the sides. Sira tried to catch one of them but her hand just scraped against the damp rugged wall. She caught a glimpse of Interpreter a bit further down and increased her pace.

"Finally, you're done! Come on! Hurry! Follow me."

Interpreter hastened away. Without having time to ask where they were heading, Sira was at his heels.

The Castle

The inhabitants of Boreal flocked to the castle. When they walked along the broad alley their breaths formed little clouds which transformed into dancing snowstars. The evening was quiet except for the crunching of the snow under their feet, hooves and skis.

Proud lantern carriers stood between the ice-covered tree trunks. Their light was reflected in the pendants of the treetops and showed the way to the castle gates. The light in the halls and windows made the castle throw a warm and inviting light towards the arriving guests. But when you came closer you could see that it was surrounded by a moat with a thin layer of ice. If you put your foot on the coating of ice it would burst and you would be sucked down into the ice-cold water and swirl around there forever. That's why it was best to cross the bridge which was lowered to welcome the inhabitants of Boreal.

Two of the Queen's guards in their best uniforms stood in front of the gates and directed the guests.

"Welcome. Please brush off the snow and then take the stairs to the left. And then go out on the big terrace."

"That's to the right. Left is that way."

"The reindeers? You don't have to worry. They will be well taken care of. We haven't had wolves or mylingar here since…"

"I beg your pardon? Gifts? No, that's not expected. You had to hurry here, did you not? That's to the right. Left is that way."

"Yes, you may keep your caps on. You're going to the terrace. Late?? That was bad. We will see what we can do…"

"Welcome. Please brush off the snow and then take the stairs to the left. That's to the right. Left is that way.

"They are already out on the terrace. They live here at the castle.

"You there, in the green. Can I have a look in your bags? We heard what happened the last time you were at a party.

"The brooms? You can put them in the cabinet over there, beside the skis.

"Exactly, the stairs to the left."

"I beg your pardon? Yes, you may continue to shine if you like. I just thought you might want to save your lights.

"That's to the right. Left is that way."

"That was that," said one of the guards and turned to the other. "That must be everybody except for the delayed."

"Yes, I told the giants to take the other entrance."

"Finally," the other guard panted and dried the sweat from his forehead. They closed the heavy gates and disappeared up to the terrace.

In the tunnels

It felt as if they had been walking in the tunnels forever. Sira was tired. First they went to the right, then to the left and then right again, then left and then straight ahead. It never seemed to end.

Sira threw a glance behind and realised that she would never find her way back. The ground under her boots crunched. Her eyes were sore from the dim lights from the little flames on the walls and the stale smell was stuck in her nose. She was close to throwing up.

"Hurry up!" urged Interpreter. We won't be able to make it if you drag your feet."

His voice sounded more and more irritated. He seemed to be as fast and indefatigable as a horse, Sira thought.

"What is it that we have to hurry to? What is this castle? What is this celebration? Why can't you tell me anything?" she asked, nearly out of breath.

"Don't ask so many questions. Hurry up instead. You will get all the answers in time."

Better do as he says, Sira said quietly to herself. *I don't want to be left alone here.*

She started half-running but stopped almost immediately. Short banging noises were heard from above and earth trickled down on her. She looked up. Somewhere far away she could hear Interpreter's warning voice calling her name. A few seconds later, she was covered in earth.

At the castle

A motley crowd was standing outside on the terrace. Long, short, thick and thin. One of the guards made them aware that the Queen waved from a small balcony almost opposite. Beside her stood two creatures. One looked like an animal they'd never seen before and the other looked like some kind of a tree, they couldn't decide which. They were also waving.

Suddenly, a star cluster appeared in the sky. It glimmered in white, red and blue. It was the constellation of the Lynx. The inhabitants of Boreal drew their breaths. Usually, the constellation of the Lynx was so weak that one needed a lynx's eyes to be able to see it. But now, it shone so strongly and clearly that everybody who saw it became enchanted. And if that wasn't enough, soon the dark parted above the Lynx and a weak-coloured light sprang forward in the firmament. The Northern Lights, Aurora Borealis, danced in a spiral of light across the sky. The weak light burst into the form of a draped dress in green, white and violet which spun and moved around the Lynx.

The glimmering star cluster seemed to follow in the dance. At intervals, Aurora Borealis formed large circles which with a strong, crackling sound prised open again and then rolled away to join another green-white sparkling light arcade. The amazing encounter in the sky was breathtaking, yes, it was beyond all reason and it went straight into the hearts of everybody that saw it happen.

Except for the lantern carriers. To them Aurora Borealis was evil and uncanny; a threat to their own shining existence.

No one knew how long the heavenly spectacle lasted but with a final crackling sound, it ended. The Northern Lights withdrew but the constellation of the Lynx continued to shine, strongly and clearly above Boreal.

When the guards announced that dinner was served in the large dining hall, a murmur went through the crowd. None of them had ever been allowed entrance there, apart from the gnomes' secret tours. A lot of chit-chat went on about the reason for this ceremony. The gnomes gave each other meaningful looks and didn't reveal that there was a wedding at hand.

On their way into the dining hall they had to pass two wolves which guarded each side of the entrance with their open hungry jaws. Some shuddered at the wolves' threatening presence while others admired their cleverly carved ice bodies.

As they crossed the threshold, they were met by a marvellous sight. Big chandeliers made with elk and reindeer horns with hundreds of candles in the ceiling and even more glimmering candle holders along the walls, lit up the cool dining hall and created a warm welcoming atmosphere. Three rows with four tables in each was set with glasses and porcelain of the finest ice glistened in the candlelight. Beside every plate there was a set of knife, fork and spoon made of the best reindeer horn and a napkin of the finest linen.

On the well-polished floor, beautiful reindeer skins were sewn together and formed passages to and between the tables.

A minor hullabaloo started when everybody tried to find their seats and the inhabitants of Boreal pushed each other here and there but without ruining the set tables.

The little gnomes, who were the only children in Boreal, had difficulty in climbing the chairs but the falor soon realised their problem and lifted them up. They were neatly combed underneath the caps, and their parents had tied a red belt around their waists which made their grey clothes a bit brighter. Their big eyes looked at everything that was happening around them. They loved the candles in the chandeliers, the candelabras on the tables and the candle holders on the walls. At home they only had weak gnome lights but here they could see everything. Never before had anything so exciting happened to them.

The dwarves' seats were near the entrance. One could see that there was something wrong. Not all of them were in place. One of them was missing which was a bad omen, especially on a night like this.

A silence full of expectation entered the dining hall. The Queen, who sat at a table with her allies on an elevated plateau far in the dining hall, rose. Everybody's eyes fell on her and gossiping started at the tables.

"How beautiful she is," one of the dwarfs sighed. "I've never seen such a blue and shimmering dress in my whole life."

"What a wonderful blue sapphire. A necklace like that is to die for," another dwarf said in an envious tone.

"I'd rather die for that silver crown. Never seen any so well-polished and with so many crystals," said yet another voice dreamily.

"I'd like to have that long raven-black plait with eagle feathers which looks like a snake wriggling over her shoulder."

"Look at her mantle, so white and so soft," Mother gnome whispered.

"Yes, it comes from Mantola, the oldest snow leopard. May she rest in peace. I'm sure she's proud that the Queen is now carrying her beautiful fur," Father gnome replied with a warm voice.

The gnomes smiled slyly. They were now totally convinced that a wedding was to be announced even if they couldn't see any consort. Because it couldn't be the one with a big thick fur or that tall tree-like figure who sat at her table. But of course there was an empty chair at the table and actually another one…

Maybe the consort would come later when the Queen had made her speech. The gnomes winked at each other and thought that it must be so.

The Queen's warm gaze wandered across the gathered. Everybody went quiet. Her voice was strong when she spoke.

"Welcome, inhabitants of Boreal! It's a great moment for me to have you all gathered here. Tonight we have witnessed something historical. The constellation of the Lynx has shown itself and together with Aurora Borealis have given us a spectacular heavenly spectacle."

Laughter, whistles and applause spread in the big dining hall but were soon quieted by the Queen's raised hand.

"I understand that you feel in high spirits over this." She smiled and continued, "But you should know that this didn't happen by chance. It is also a sign. It's been a thousand years since the Lynx showed itself so strong and clear to the eye and then our history changed. Tonight it's happening again which means that our history is about to change once more. That's why you are here. And we have very special guests here tonight."

A hiss of surprise rose and everybody looked around the hall.

"Here at my table, The Powerful, the Illustrious and the Ethereal are seated," the Queen said. "And we're awaiting a fourth guest. You must wonder who that could be and it is a truly special guest, seldom seen here in

Boreal. Let us now eat together and propose a toast to Boreal."

The Queen raised her glass:

"To Boreal!"

"To Boreal!" the voices echoed in the hall and the different colours of the glasses glistened as they were reflected in the candlelight.

The Queen sat down and voices buzzed around the tables.

The lantern carriers muttered something about Aurora Borealis and their lights went out one by one. They felt deeply disappointed because the Queen hadn't mentioned their shining contributions in her speech.

The discussions about the guests were loud around the tables. Especially who the fourth very special guest might be. *Seldom seen...* did it mean that the guest had been here before but a long, long time ago? Maybe a thousand years ago? Or had the guest never visited Boreal before? They were like a group of Nosey Parkers.

Moltas the dwarf

The table-setters started to serve the first course which was thin slices of bear meat on some fir sprigs. Before you started to eat you had to pull the meat through a brass ring. This was done so as not to catch the bear shiver. The bear would give them the power to see their inner strength and the courage to show it. But the bear also had a dangerous and evil side. Therefore, so as not to get that evil inside of you, you had to pull the meat through a brass ring before you ate it. There were stories about those who hadn't and they became lame from head to toe. Their voices had remained but the only sound that came out of their mouths were bear roars and they had stayed that way for the rest of their lives.

"You're late Moltas! You missed the whole thing," his elder brother Nilas said when Moltas entered the dining hall. With his cap on the side, sweat on his forehead and his beard full of snow stars, he climbed up on the chair.

"Lucky for you that the Queen didn't notice that you weren't here," another dwarf said.

Moltas didn't seem to listen and threw himself into the first course. He loved the wild and strong taste of bear meat. Moltas' sister, Elle, who sat opposite him, realised what was happening but before she could open her mouth it was too late. Moltas had already swallowed it all. Elle screamed. Her short broad finger pointed at Moltas and everybody turned to him. But Moltas neither saw nor heard.

He wiped his mouth, took a sip of ancient water and then he noticed that everybody was staring at him.

"Moltas forgot the brass ring. He forgot to pull the bea—I mean Goldfoot through the brass ring!" she shouted.

The dwarf's eyes turned black. Moltas shrank.

"How could you do that? You're such a careless thing! First, you're late and then you forget the brass ring," Nilas said and shook his head.

"I was so hungry. I forgot," answered Moltas and felt tears sting in his eyes.

"What a nuisance. What shall we do?" said one of Moltas' cousins and wrung his hands.

They were all in a state.

"We have to tell the Queen," said the cousin, upset. "She won't be happy," another cousin filled in.

Moltas' stomach twisted.

I will go to the Queen before the main course is served. Maybe we can save—" began Elle.

"Wait a minute!" said Nilas and rose from his seat.

"Moltas, you know that when the peregrines come it's important to be on time," he continued and couldn't help feeling a bit sorry for his brother.

Tears streamed down Moltas' round cheeks and gathered like raindrops in his curly beard.

"The sky was so beautiful and I thought I would get a better view if I climbed Akka," he sobbed.

"Did you climb to the top of Akka? You silly! It's at least five miles from home," said Nilas, irritated.

Everybody looked accusingly at Moltas who blushed. He put his hand in his pocket. "I found this at the top."

They all went quiet as he held up a black tuft of hair. Nilas leaned forward to get a closer look and cried:

"A tuft of hair from a lynx!"

"Where did you say you found it?" asked one of the cousins while he studied the thin black tuft of hair with great interest.

"At the top."

"Do you remember exactly where at the top you found it?" the cousin asked as his eyes nearly popped out of his head.

"On the black stone."

"Can I hold it, please Moltas?" asked another cousin.

"No!" said Elle. "It was Moltas who found it."

"You said you found it on the big black stone. Tell us more," said Nilas curiously.

"I had just reached the top," Moltas began. "It was amazing! All the colours dancing in the sky…" Moltas gazed dreamily into the distance.

"We know! Tell us now what happened when you got the tuft of hair."

"I had just reached the top of Akka…" Moltas continued.

Everybody was so eager to know and leaned further and further across the table.

"We've already heard that. What happened next?" shouted some of them.

"My clothes were full of snow so I had to brush it off. I even had snow inside my jumper. Guess if it was cold to my stomach!"

"Get on, Moltas!" they urged.

"When I was on top of the stone and was sitting down, the stone felt both soft and hard at the same time and it moved. I got frightened actually."

"Ugh! How scary!" Elle shivered.

"I reached out my hand to keep my balance and got hold of something soft. Right then one of the stars in the sky shone blue. And then I saw that I sat on the back of a lynx holding one of its ears."

A hiss of expectation was heard around the table.

"The lynx turned its head and looked at me. Then it rose and I fell off with the tuft of hair still in my hand."

Moltas opened his hand and everybody's eyes fell on the black tuft of hair which looked so big in his little hand.

"What did it do after that? Did it bite you?" asked a cousin and showed his teeth.

"At first I thought it would as the tuft of hair had come off and it might think it was my fault," answered Moltas.

"But it just jumped down from the stone and disappeared."

It became quiet around the table. Everybody looked at Moltas with deep admiration. Moltas squirmed a little, uncomfortable with all the attention. He had still caused trouble by arriving late and forgetting the brass ring. This tuft of hair wasn't that special, was it? He had only climbed Akka to be able to see the sky better.

"Imagine that! You got the tuft of hair from the lynx's ear," said Nilas with a pleased look.

"Oh, I'm so proud of you," Elle said and little stars glimmered in her big blue eyes. Moltas felt a bit better from all the attention but he didn't tell the other dwarves that an icing chill crept up his spine.

The leprechauns play pranks

Father gnome and Mother gnome were very pleased with the little gnomes' good behaviour. There was only one cloud hanging over them and that was leprechauns' pranks. You never knew what they could be up to.

"Mum, Mum! He's throwing things at our table."

A small rainbow came bouncing across the table and landed in one of the little gnome's glasses. The little gnome stared fascinated at all the colours which jumped up and down in his glass. He wanted so badly to taste the rainbow which swam among the cranberries.

"Stop! Don't drink…!"

But the little gnome had already taken a sip and all of sudden his clothes had the colours of the rainbow. Mother gnome turned angrily at the leprechauns' table where they were doubled up with laughter and she realised that it was not a good idea to talk to them. She turned to the little gnomes:

"If they throw any more things in your glasses you mustn't drink it. Understood?!"

All the little gnomes nodded earnestly. Mother gnome sighed.

Father gnome said: "My dearest, we must try to put up with it. It's a very special evening and we can't disappoint the Queen by going home. And I know that you wouldn't miss this evening for anything in the world."

Father gnome smiled secretly at his wife who couldn't help raise a corner of her mouth.

"Yes, I know but those leprechauns are so full of mischief. They're always making—"

"Mother, Mother! My pockets are full of silver coins! I can keep them, can't I? Please, Mother," said one of the boys.

"No, you cannot. They're not yours. We must give them back at once!"

Mother gnome took the silver coins and was just about to hand them back when they suddenly turned into a broom. Even angrier than the last time, she turned to the leprechauns' table where they were twice doubled up with laughter. When she was about to jump down from her chair and go to their table the broom turned into lots of small rainbows which bounced around on the table. Before she could do anything, the rainbows ended up in the little gnomes' glasses and they all hurried to drink them. A moment later, their clothes showed all the colours of the rainbow. The little gnomes were overjoyed and their parents in despair.

"Indeed, that's enough!"

Mother gnome stared at the leprechauns and they hadn't stopped laughing.

"Calm down, dear. Now you've warned them twice and we all know what will happen the third time," Father gnome said and took Mother gnome's hand and gave her a soothing glance. She leaned back and wiped her forehead with the elegant napkin.

"You're perfectly right, my dear husband. I hope the main course will arrive soon or I'll get a headache."

Suddenly, the sound of breaking crystal glasses was heard. Everybody stopped what they were doing and turned apprehensively to look at the leprechauns' table. Father gnome sighed.

"Oh well, now you see, children, what happens when you don't follow the rules, like pulling Goldfoot through the brass ring."

He pointed at the leprechauns.

"Why do you always have to say Goldfoot when it's bea—?" The little girl quickly went quiet when her big sister pinched her arm.

"Mother and father have already told you a hundred times! You mustn't say the right word because bad things can happen and we can get into trouble, stupid!"

The big sister let go of her sister's arm and Father gnome looked admonishingly at his younger daughter.

The little gnomes stared horrified at the green-clad leprechauns. They were terrified that something bad was going to happen and it would.

The bear shiver had its grip on the leprechauns. Beads of sweat on their foreheads rolled down into their wrinkles and became ice. Their pointed ears got ice crystal earrings and their three-cornered hats froze onto their heads. One after one they became stiff and frozen and a bear roar crawled inside of them. As their faces had frozen in the middle of a laughter, you couldn't see how scared they really were. Mother and Father gnome had their hands full trying to comfort the little ones who cried because they thought it was going to happen to them as well.

The Bear shiver

When this happened the table-clearers had just finished and the table-setters had just begun the service of the main course. But the atmosphere in the hall was uneasy. The service of the main course was called off and a couple of table-clearers were sent in haste to the Queen's table. Two chairs were empty. The Queen wasn't there. The Illustrious, the Ethereal and the Powerful were busy with the main course, which they already had been served.

"Hrm, hrm. Excuse us for bothering you. We would like to speak to the Queen. It's very important. Bear shiver!"

The Illustrious, the Powerful and the Ethereal stopped eating and looked surprised at the two table-clearers.

"Bear shiver, you said? That sounds very serious."

The Illustrious frowned and scratched lightly with one of its claws on the table. A sprinkle of spit came from the Ethereal.

"The Queen is not here at the moment. She had to leave and we can't say exactly when she will be back," the Powerful said and glanced rather worriedly at the Illustrious.

"What do we do?" The table-clearers looked at each other.

"The bear shiver has already taken its grip on the leprechauns and one of the dwarves. It might spread if we don't stop it. I have heard that—"

The table-clearer was interrupted by the Illustrious, which put its paw on the table-clearer's head, so that he almost fell to the floor from its weight.

"Calm down. I know the Queen had hoped that this would not happen but she has calculated that it might. Glasses with beaten bear gall and bear blood are placed on a tray in the kitchen. Hurry and bring them the antidote now."

The table-clearer bowed and hurried to give the antidote to the naughty leprechauns and the forgetful dwarf Moltas. One by one they had to drink up the disgusting contents of the glass. It would take a while before it had any effect, if it had any at all. You couldn't be too sure. Some stories told that there were those that the antidote didn't have any effect on who became lame and roared like bears until they died.

"Hopefully, the antidote will help. The dwarf was probably just careless but what is distressing is the leprechauns' behaviour. They are too unreliable. We really don't have time for this," the Illustrious said and sipped some water.

"No we don't. I hope they didn't think too much about the Queen's absence." The Powerful fumbled for its fork and a dried leaf fell from a twig onto its plate. The Ethereal blew it away.

Coughing was heard from the leprechauns. They began to come out of the horrifying experience. For some of them the bear roar was stuck in their throats and when their voices worked again, they began to sound like angry bears. Everybody in the dining hall stared horrified at them, especially the little gnomes and several of them started to cry again.

But within seconds, one fala threw the rune Iss through the air. The sticklike icicle first hit the leprechauns and then Moltas. The beginning bear roars fell silent. Iss flew back to its place in the fala's bag and the leprechauns and Moltas had soon recovered. The table-setters continued serving the main course, which consisted of elk meatloaf with mashed potatoes and preserved lingonberry jam. The elk's meat would give the inhabitants of Boreal pride and decisiveness. But the elk, like the bear, had a dangerous and evil side. So as not to catch that evil you mustn't say the elk's proper name but call it 'Longlegs'. And that was for the best, because if you happened to call it by its proper name, bumps of horn could grow on your head and you would never be healthy again. The most frightful story was told about someone who forgot himself and was forced to gore his horn bumpy head against a tree and bellow like a wounded elk for the rest of his life.

The bear shiver and the bear roars had given everybody a real fright and the main course was eaten in silence. But as far as the leprechauns was concerned it didn't last long. Soon their thawed fingers started to itch and their sly looks shone like emeralds when they looked around the dining hall. Who should they play a prank on now?

In the tunnels

Sira was covered in earth from head to toe. She didn't dare to move. The roars and the screams from above were horrifying and jarred upon her ears. The banging too.

Finally she had to move. Her eyes and ears were filled with earth and she felt desperate for a breath of air. She managed to free her arm and swept her hand over her face, sneezed and coughed. Flapping sounds came from above soon followed by penetrating screams. She felt sharp claws tearing her coat, her trousers, in trying to dig her out. Shortly after she felt a thud close by; the piercing screams ended and something heavy landed on her legs. Everything went black.

"Sira! Sira!" Can you hear me? Sira?" Somebody called her name while fighting to dig her out. A hauling, sliding sound freed her legs and she could move her feet. She tried to place the voice. Who was it?

"Sira! Wake up, Sira! Someone pulled her out of the mound of earth.

"I'm awake. What's happening?" She sat up and opened her eyes. Interpreter's thin eyes stared at her.

"Where am I? Is that really you, Interpreter? I recognise your voice but not your eyes." She coughed and spat again.

"We must get out of here quickly before they come back. Can you stand up?" Interpreter tried to help her but she fell down again. Screams and flapping sounds came from a distance.

"You have to get up Sira! You *have* to. They'll be returning soon. If they catch us we won't be able to make it."

Interpreter grabbed her hands and pulled as hard as he could. Large pearls of sweat ran down his face. But he didn't want to use his sleeve to wipe them off, instead he used his hand which left streaks of dirt all over his otherwise perfectly clean face.

Sira fought and managed to get on her feet at last. But was it too late? It was unbearably quiet. Heavy flapping sounds came closer. Interpreter snatched her hand and she almost tripped over something in front of her.

She bent down and saw a big black bird with broken wings at her feet. Was it a raven? The half-open beak was hard and bent with grey bumps on. A rough grey and yellowish tongue stuck out. Sira felt sick from the nasty smell. Interpreter grabbed her and they ran as fast as they could. The flapping sound faded away and Interpreter stopped. Sira caught her breath.

"It was close or worse," Interpreter said.

"What actually happened?" Sira asked.

"You don't want to know but I can tell you we narrowly avoided your death. Don't ask more. Come, we're almost at the castle."

Sira was terrified but did as Interpreter told her. She followed him and didn't ask any more questions. A short while after, as they rounded the corner, a shape appeared with open arms in front of them.

"There you are, finally! I was beginning to doubt that you would make it."

"Yes, mylingar almost got her but we managed to get away," Interpreter said while he adjusted his uniform and wiped some pearls of sweat from his forehead. He pushed Sira forward.

"My Queen, allow me to introduce Sira."

The Queen smiled and her warm ice-blue eyes met Sira's bewildered brown eyes.

"Welcome Sira. Welcome to Boreal."

Sira felt like a question mark and couldn't say a word.

"I understand that you are wondering who I am and where you are and you will get all the answers to your questions in due course," said the shape who was called the Queen.

"Now I ask you to kindly and hurriedly follow me. Time is short. Interpreter will show you the way."

And before Sira blinked, the Queen disappeared.

"Come along, hurry. The Queen said that time is running out. Follow me." Interpreter ran towards a staircase and Sira could do nothing but follow.

The dinner

The dwarves finished the main course first of all. They wiped their mouths, leaned back, burped and farted and the table-clearers had to put pegs on their noses before they rolled out the dishwasher cart.

With efficient speed they cleared the plates and put them in the dishwasher cart, which was a leather bag filled with hot water so the plates melted quickly. The knives and forks were put in a small self-washing and self-drying bag, which hung on the side of the cart. As the table-clearers finished, the table-setters began serving the dessert, cloudberries with crushed ice. Cloudberries, like cranberries, were rare in Boreal and therefore a huge success among the guests.

The atmosphere was tremendous and portion after portion went down their stomachs. And that was for the best, because no one knew when cloudberries were to be served again.

One of the table-clearers bent down to Mother gnome's ear and whispered: "The Queen will speak again soon; it's time for the little ones to go to bed." He was just about to clear her plate when Mother gnome reached out with her spoon to catch the last golden cloudberry. She managed to get it onto her spoon but before it reached her mouth it turned into a frozen rainbow and teasing laughter was heard from the leprechauns' table.

"Third time lucky!" Mother gnome banged the spoon on the table, threw herself down from the chair and strode to the leprechauns' table. Her peppercorn eyes flared and with her fist in the air she shouted:

"Third time lucky:
All will be mucky.
When you get home,
Watch out for a gnome!"

The leprechauns stopped in silence and pretended to look down at the table. They knew that if you teased the gnomes too much something bad would happen. But they couldn't help themselves because angry gnomes were the best, and they didn't believe in any spells for sure. As soon as Mother gnome turned her back they began laughing and making up new pranks.

With angry strides, Mother gnome went back to her table and said to the little gnomes: "Children, it's time for bed."

"Please Mother, not yet. Can't we stay up a little longer, please?" begged one of the little gnomes.

"No, the party is over as far as you are concerned. Off to bed now, children!"

"Please Father, please, please! Can't we stay up just a little bit longer?" the little gnomes pleaded.

"You heard your mother. It's bedtime. Now off you go," said Father gnome with that wrinkle between his eyes which the little gnomes knew meant it was the end of the conversation. Silently they jumped off their chairs and hurried away.

When the little ones were out of sight, the two gnomes gave each other a meaningful look. A tingle went through them, now it was time for the wedding and very soon they would know whom the Queen was going to marry.

The little gnomes

When the little gnomes marched out of the dining hall, they looked up at the chandeliers and the many candles along the walls. As soon as the big doors closed behind them, they scurried away into another hall and stopped in front of an ice sculpture. Behind it was one of their many holes which led down to the tunnels and soon they were gone.

"It's so dark here. Why do we only have gnome candles?" one of them said.

"I wonder why too. I want to have the same candles as they have in the dining hall," said another one.

"Me too."

"Yes, they're really nice but gnome candles are good for our eyes. And we will soon be home."

The dormitory was at the end of the tunnel. It was spacious and neat with ten little beds along one wall and ten little beds along the opposite wall. Bedside tables with gnome candles stood in between the beds. The floor was covered with reindeer skins and in one corner there were lots of soft pillows.

Above each bed hung a small dream catcher with the purpose of sorting out bad dreams. Tonight someone had hung up new dream catchers. Boreal's one and only

Spider mother, which was very famous and sought-after, had had busy days weaving new nets of airy ice crystals. Its frame was a ring of purified ice. Stones and pearls were woven into the net which gave each dream catcher a unique and very beautiful pattern. In the middle of each net was a hole with a shimmering rock crystal within. Three strings of sinew hung at the bottom, each of them strung with a pearl and a feather.

"Look! We have got new dream catchers. They're so pretty."

The youngest little gnomes jumped up on their beds, held up their arms and tried to reach the feathers.

"I can't!"

"Me neither. Why?"

"I just want to feel the feathers a little. They look so soft."

"Why is it so hard?"

The tiny hands waved helplessly in the air.

"Wait, let me have a look."

The oldest little gnome, Lea, jumped up on her bed and reached for the dream catcher. She was tall enough to reach it but still it was like her hand couldn't touch it.

"How strange." Lea tried to feel in the air around it to see if she could find an opening. "It seems like there's an invisible bubble around it. No, I can't."

She jumped down from the bed.

"Pooh! We'll wait until tomorrow," said the second-oldest gnome, Nol. "Maybe the bubble will be gone by then."

"I know," said Lea. "Tonight we've seen the Lynx in the sky and if everybody sits down here, then you, Nol, can tell us something about the real lynx, can't you?" Nol's face brightened up and everybody hurried to sit down.

"The lynx is actually one of my favourite animals. It's—"

"It's mine too."

"Mine also."

"And mine."

Nol cleared his throat and said:

"As I was going to say, it's a huge animal with black spots on—"

"We know what it looks like, Nol!" they all said in one voice. "Tell us something exciting instead."

"Okay. The lynx often wanders alone. It has a large habitat all of its own where it preys on reindeer and other animals, which it eats. A flesh-eater so to speak. It also has a secret name, Goepan. The horrible thing about the lynx is that it can tear you into little pieces and eat you in a flash. But only if it gets angry, really angry. And no one here wants to meet a lynx that is angry, do you?"

They all huddled together. There was silence in the room.

"But if you ever do, you'd better know the lynx's secret name, Goepan. Because then you can say a spell which goes like this," said Nol and got to his feet.

"Goepan, Goepan, Goepan
You mustn't be mad.

Or I will turn into wolf,
And that will be very sad.

And then you show your teeth," recited Nol showing his teeth and everybody jumped.

"And then the lynx will be so scared and run away as fast as it can. Because the wolf is strong and hunts in a pack and they could easily kill it."

"Is there anything good about the lynx or at least not so scary anyway?" asked one of the youngest little gnomes.

Nol thought for a while.

"As a matter of fact there is. I can tell you about its ear tufts. They are like antennas which absorb all the magic information from the universe. And they help the lynx to hear secrets better. If you're lucky enough to get close to a lynx's ears you can hear them tell something secret and magic."

"But doesn't the lynx get angry if you get too close?"

"Yes, it can but then you can use the spell."

"It's bedtime now," Lea interrupted and got up to help her younger siblings to bed. "It was exciting to listen to you, Nol."

They all kept their rainbow-coloured clothes on when they got into bed. And that was for the best, for they knew for sure that their mother wouldn't allow them to keep them on the next day. The oldest little gnomes blew out the candles. And it didn't take long before you could hear how they slept and sniffed.

The Queen's speech

Reluctantly, Interpreter sat down at the giants' table. He thought they were unkempt with their long, tangled hair and dirty frayed coats. He wondered why they had to be there as they didn't understand anything and nobody could talk to them. But the Queen had insisted on everybody attending this evening and his mission was to be their translator.

"Why cast pearls before swine?" he muttered and brushed off some snowflakes from his uniform. A couple of giants rattled their glasses and Interpreter rubbed his medal which read: *For The Best Interpretation Ever.* He sighed and dreamt away about better missions. And it didn't take long before a glass fell on the floor and he was forced to translate to them that this evening was very important and they had to exert themselves not to disturb the other guests. Their big, round eyes turned to him and he realised that they hadn't understood what he meant, even though he had spoken their mother tongue and used multicultural gestures.

Impatience bubbled inside of him and just when he was going to blurt out a rigmarole which would put them in place, the Queen rose and the dining hall became full of expectation.

"Dear inhabitants of Boreal, I hope the food was to your liking."

Applause and laughter all around the dining hall.

"It is a great honour to have you all gathered here tonight."

Even more clapping and laughter.

"But I also have sad news for you and I will get straight to the point: Everybody here remembers Elakka."

Dead silence. Even the giants and leprechauns stopped being noisy.

"Everybody remembers Elakka and what she did many long years ago. And it is with a heavy heart I must tell you that Elakka is free and…"

The Queen fumbled with the words. "… and destruction is closing in on us."

Despair, cries and horror filled the dining hall.

"I understand that this message comes as an unpleasant surprise. And we must stop her. We must destroy her before she destroys us and ruins the whole of Boreal! But… there is hope." The Queen paused. "What you have witnessed tonight, the heavenly spectacle, is a sign. A sign that help is on its way. Because we have to stop her, destroy her before she destroys us!"

An anxious murmur of voices passed between the tables.

"Inhabitants of Boreal!" she said in a loud voice to quiet the guests. "We must do everything in our power to find Elakka and bring her back to the Big Mountain again. Or rather, destroy her!"

Weak applause.

"I said earlier that we have a special guest with us tonight." A big light hit the Queen's table. "Apart from the Ethereal, the Powerful and the Illustrious, I would like to introduce Sira."

Sira was blinded by the light cast straight at her. Despite the glaring light, she saw all the guests staring at her with open mouths. Sira blushed from all the attention and looked down at the table.

Interpreter, who had left the giants' table to support Sira, nudged her side and whispered that she had to stand up.

The Queen held out her arms towards Sira:

"As you can see, Sira is human. We have never before had a visit from a human in Boreal, so you must realise how serious this is. Sira is one of few humans who still has her imagination left and the only human who can help us to catch Elakka."

Sira thought how small she was standing beside the Queen. She felt the ground shake beneath her feet and her head spun. Somewhere far away she heard the Queen's voice. Did this really happen? Where was she? Not long ago she was at home in Backaviken. And now in Boreal? What sort of country was this Boreal? A place where fairy-tale characters like gnomes, leprechauns, giants, dwarves and other figures lived? No, such figures didn't exist. Or…? Moreover, the Queen claimed that she, Sira, was the only one who could help them find someone called Elakka!

Everything went black before her eyes and she fell helplessly backwards.

The black hole

When the night came, the constellation of the Lynx changed. It shone even more brightly and strongly. Like the beat of a heart, it contracted and dilated while at the same time pumped out small balls of white, green and blue light in abundance. They spread across the sky faster than the speed of light itself; towards east, west, south and towards north, towards Boreal.

When the balls approached the castle they formed the shape of a long tail. Like a flying snake, it wriggled through the chinks in the castle. Inside the castle it wound, searching. In one of the halls it found a hole in the floor which it went through. It dwindled through the passages and when it found the little gnomes dormitory it turned into balls again. A weak gust of wind put the dream catchers in motion and when the balls hit them, one by one, the rock stone in the middle glimmered. And the balls evaporated. The unsuspecting little gnomes slept peacefully and if you were watching them, you would have seen little smiles on their lips. On everybody's lips except for Nol's. He tossed and turned when the dreams came to him.

All the little gnomes were in deep sleep when the hour of the wolf tolled and none of them heard when the four gnomes crept on tiptoe into the dormitory. Their grey clothes and woollen caps made them look like shadows against the icy wall.

"It's time to clean the dream catchers again," said Bol and unfolded a ladder by one of the beds. He climbed up and took down the dream catcher carefully.

"Here, catch," said Bol and handed over the dream catcher to Bal.

"How unusually beautiful this is. The Spider mother is very clever. But look how much dirt it has caught this time," said Bal.

"It must be the worst we have seen. It'll be a lot of work cleaning all these. We'd better get started."

Bol climbed down in a jiffy and hurried away with the ladder to the next bed.

"I wonder if it has anything to do with the constellation of the Lynx showing itself tonight?" said Bil.

"What do you mean?" asked Bul.

"I'm only thinking, new dream catcher this very night. And all this extra garbage."

"You have a point. But on the other hand, we were wrong when we thought that the dinner was held because the Queen was to marry Justice."

Bol chuckled quietly.

"Instead it got worse. Elakka free. Can you imagine anything badder?" Bil said.

"You can't say 'badder'. You say 'worse'. Actually. But we haven't always been wrong, have we? Do you remember when—"

Bal was interrupted.

"Yuck! What horrific stuff! Can you push the garbage mixer over here, please?" said Bul.

"Of course, here it comes," answered Bal and gave a rectangular box on wheels a push across the room.

"Be quiet! Don't wake the children. The lid is stuck."

Bul had to use both hands to force the lid up.

"Down with you. Ugh! Horrible garbage!" A slurping sound was heard when the garbage mixer started.

"What's stuck in here, in Nol's dream catcher? Come and have a look!" said Bil. The other three gnomes rushed to Nol's bed.

"Ugh! A hole. Totally black. And it's moving!" said Bal.

"Here, quickly, put it in the mixer and start it at once!" said Bul.

"Wait! I want to have a look at it first," said Bol.

"Why? No, let's throw it away now. We don't know what it consists of," said Bal.

"I want to have a peek inside first. Give it to me," said Bol and reached for the hole.

"Okay, but be quick and then we'll throw it away," said Bul.

"Don't put your whole head in it!" said Bil.

"I'm not, but it looks like something is stuck inside, something round and shiny—a ball maybe. You must help me to hold the hole so I can reach it."

The gnomes fought to hold the hole still. But when Bol stretched out his arms, the hole swallowed and the round, shiny ball went further inside. Bol stretched himself even more and the hole swallowed again.

"Help! What happened?" said Bul, terrified.

"He went straight in, didn't you see?" said Bal.

The hole landed on the floor and tried to roll towards the open door.

"Catch it!" Bil shouted.

The gnomes threw themselves towards it but the black hole was faster and before anyone could wink it disappeared through the open door. And if you listened carefully, you could hear cawing and screaming sounds coming from it as it rolled away from the castle.

Some of the little gnomes sobbed.

"Oh no! Not that as well. We must make them go to sleep again."

The gnomes rushed to the crying little gnomes. They patted their foreheads, dried their tears, whispered something in their ears and tucked them up. And soon they were asleep again.

The three gnomes sat down.

"What are we going to do? I told you we should put it in the garbage mixer directly. But Bol is too curious. And look now what happened." Bal pulled his cap down over his eyes.

"What are we going to do? What can we do? He's gone!" said Bil and bit his thin yellow nails.

"Stop biting your nails. We've to take care of the rest of the dream catchers before dawn otherwise the nightmares can cling to the children forever."

Bul got on his feet.

"But we must also tell the Queen what's happened. What if everything is our fault. It's our fault that the black hole took Bol with it and disappeared."

"Let's clean up first and tell the Queen later," said Bal.

They worked fast with cleaning the rest of the dream catchers and didn't complain even though it was hard work getting them clean. When everything was done they made sure that the lid on the garbage mixer was securely fastened. While it made its slurping sound, they put all the dream catchers back in place above the beds. Then they tiptoed out of the dormitory.

The Chosen

"Finally, you're awake, Sira. We have been waiting." Interpreter gave her an impatient look.

"Come, hurry up! You play a big part in the plan."

Sira sat up and she got confused when she met Interpreter's eyes. She was in a bed covered with reindeer skins. Lowered voices were heard from an adjacent room.

Sira coughed. "What plan? Where am I?" She got more and more angry. "Can't anyone tell me where I am? A short time ago I was at home, in the woods. I was only going to run away from Mum for a little while. She never cares about me. She just works all the time and…"

She burst into tears. At once you could sense a glimpse of compassion from the Interpreter.

"Now then. It's because…" He stopped speaking abruptly and turned to the other room where the voices came from.

"Come now, Sira. There is no time to lose."

Sira stood up and followed Interpreter to the adjacent room. The cold which made her tighten her coat, didn't seem to bother those sitting around the table in the middle of the room. Her breath shaped small white stars which floated upwards towards the ceiling. Her eyes followed them and caught the most beautiful chandelier she had ever seen. Intertwined horns from elk and reindeer shaped into a huge ball, and inside the ball gleamed at least a thousand little crystals and candles which gave the room a pleasant light.

Sira lowered her eyes and let them wander around the room. Instantly, they met a pair of yellow eyes. Sira winced, closed her eyes for a second but when she opened them again, the pair of yellow eyes were still there, staring at her. It was a lynx standing in one of the corners. Sira's gaze wandered and she drew in her breath when she noticed that a wolf with blue, staring eyes and open jaws standing in another corner. In every corner there was an animal staring at her. She closed her eyes and swallowed and thought that this was her last moment. Interpreter patted her back.

"The beasts are not alive, Sira. You can calm down," he said and went to the wolf and put his fur- skinned glove in its open jaws.

"They are all ice sculptures and are they not cleverly made?" he continued.

"Welcome Sira! Come and sit over here," said a voice at the table.

Sira was pulled out of her panic and put her coat straight. She walked to the table and Interpreter was pulled out one of the fur-lined chairs for her, thereafter he sat himself beside her. Quickly, she was served a glass of water with something that looked like lingonberries jumping up and down in it.

"Drink Sira. You must be thirsty. Are you hungry?"

Sira didn't feel hungry but very thirsty. She turned to the voice that spoke to her.

"I met you before. You are the Queen. We were at a dinner and you spoke of someone called Elakka and something about me being one of few who still have imagination left. And that I am the only human who can help you find Elakka? What does it all mean?"

The Queen looked deep into her eyes. The big blue sapphire around her neck glistened.

"You will have all your answers in time. First, I would like you to meet the Powerful, the Illustrious and the Ethereal. It was them who sat at the table in the large dining hall. And of course, Interpreter, whom you have already met."

The Queen smiled. The gathered rose and bowed as she introduced them. Sira looked surprised at the Ethereal's chair when it was pulled out from the table and then pushed back again.

The animal reminded her of a lion with its big jaws and enormous paws. The Powerful looked like an old tree with sharp knotty branches and the Ethereal, well, what could you say about that one? Sira smiled at the thought of being invisible. What would that feel like?

"We have gathered here because Boreal is in great danger and we need your help. I understand that imagination is disappearing from you humans."

"You mean …?" Sira thought back. It was true. Her grandmother was the only person who still could come up with and tell stories. Neither Mum nor the art teacher had any imagination. "You're right," said Sira and met the eyes of the Queen. "My mother has become a different person since the divorce from my father. Before, she used to come with me to grandmother's house and sit beside me when grandmother told stories but now she's working all the time. That's why I ran away. I ran through the woods on my way to my grandmother's house—"

The Queen interrupted. "And then you ended up here. Everything has a meaning. We will help each other, Sira. Elakka was once the Mistress of Boreal. I say, *was* the Mistress, because what she did to Boreal can never be forgiven. Many years ago she was banned from Boreal and fettered deep inside a mountain. Just recently we have found out that she has managed to escape and it is of great importance that we find her as soon as possible."

"What has she done that can never be forgiven? It must be something really bad." Sira shivered.

"There is no time to dig deeper into that matter. The important thing is that…"

Everybody's eyes turned to the crystal ball standing in the middle of the table. Inside of it, the dim ice sculptures changed shapes and the room became colder. The twisted, scornful face of Elakka turned up. Out of her toothless mouth gushed frost which formed the letters **REVENGE!** on the inside of the glass.

Sira felt how everything suddenly stopped. She tried to move, talk but she couldn't. The distorted face changed, turned into mylingar which flew around on ravens, shouting and banging on the inside of the crystal ball. The Queen hurried to cup her hands around it. The shouting and banging stopped and when she took away her hands the mylingar were gone. Everybody drew a breath of relief and Sira could move again.

"Was that Elakka? And the other horrible creatures which flew around, what were they? I couldn't move. It was scary."

"Yes, that was Elakka in person. And the others were mylingar. They are Elakka's spies and they ride around on ravens. They see and hear everything and report back to Elakka."

"Mylingar, I think I've heard that name before…"

The Queen nodded as she said, "They are very dangerous. It was them that nearly killed you when you ran in the woods. You were lucky that the gnomes saved you just in time. It was mylingar that attacked you and Interpreter in the tunnels."

She turned to Interpreter:

"Interpreter, you were very brave and we are deeply grateful that you managed to bring Sira to us." The others around the table nodded in agreement.

Interpreter blushed and he stroke the medal on his chest: *For The Best Interpretation Ever.*

"I only did my best and we were lucky that we were close to the castle."

"Hmhm, is it not better that we get on with the plan now?" The Illustrious scratched one of its claws on the table.

"Of course. Now that we are all here and—"

"Excuse me, my Queen." A guard entered the room and looked around nervously. "Two of the gnomes wish to speak to the Queen. And it seems to be very urgent." The guard looked pale.

"Send them in at once," answered the Queen.

Presently the two gnomes, Bal and Bul, stood in front of the Queen with their caps in their hands. They made obeisance to the Queen.

"Excuse us for disturbing our Queen."

"Yes, excuse us for disturbing our Queen but something terrible has happened."

"Something very terrible has happened. Our deepest apology to our Queen."

"Yes, we want to apologise. We didn't mean to. We tried to stop him but he's so stubborn."

"He's really stubborn and now... Now he's gone."

"What do you mean? What has happened? Who is gone?" asked the Queen. The two gnomes looked at each other.

"You tell the Queen."

"Me? Okay. It happened when we were cleaning the dream catchers. We found a black hole in Nol's dream catcher."

"A black hole?"

"Yes, and it sort of lived. It moved. Our friend Bol, who's gone now, couldn't help but look inside it even though we said that he shouldn't."

"And what happened to him?"

"He disappeared straight into it. The hole landed on the floor and rolled towards the door. We did everything we could to stop it but it was too fast. And we couldn't get hold of it."

Bal gave Bul a nudge with his elbow.

"We couldn't get hold of it but that wasn't the worstest. The worstest was that it seemed to be something or someone inside the black hole. And we think that our friend Bol might be eaten by now. That he'll never come back…"

Both gnomes got tears in their peppercorn eyes. The Queen reached out her hands and patted them on their cheeks.

"Everything will be all right. I will make sure that we find Bol. Hurry back now."

She nudged the two gnomes towards the door and they scurried away. The Queen sighed and looked worried.

"It sounds like Elakka has used mylingar to get into the castle. The black hole, it must have been them. And they have taken one of ours… And we do not know why the black hole got stuck in one of the dreamcatchers. We do not have any time to lose now. We have to put the plan into action. We must catch Elakka before it is too late!"

She looked around the room. "Guard! We cannot be disturbed under any circumstances. Leave us."

The guard made a quick obeisance to the Queen and left. The others leaned across the table and listened carefully to the Queen's plan.

"…and to be safe you must travel in two different groups. It is best if the little gnomes travel by themselves and you by yourselves. In that way, hopefully, we can trick Elakka's spies."

The others nodded.

"Then you will meet up here." She pointed at the map.

"I have been told that Elakka is in the Black Mountain. As you can see it is not far away from your meeting place."

The crystal ball glimmered in a mumbling of voices and during the night, the plan would be put into action.

Ruvoj och Spraettarna

The stars shone bright. It snowed lightly. No one saw the giant Skade skiing away from the castle. Her bow and quiver hung on her right shoulder . The handmade rucksack of reindeer skin jolted on her back. And in the rucksack sat Sira, Interpreter, Father and Mother gnome. It wasn't a very comfortable way to travel but it was the best. No one could see or detect them. Skade was fast and confident on her skis and to help her, a lantern carrier which sat astride her shoulders and lit up the way in front of her. And that was needed because it was very dark. The crystal ball had shown that Elakka was inside of the Black Mountain many long, giant strides from the castle and even if Skade maintained a high speed, it would take a long time to get there.

Inside the rucksack they sat on a soft reindeer skin holding a leather string in their hands. The leather had a pleasant smell.

"How it jogs and jumps in here." Father gnome pulled a face and tightened his grip around the string.

"And it's so dark," Mother gnome whispered and put her free hand on Father gnome's leg. She thought about her little gnomes. For their safety, the Queen wanted them to travel on their own and Mother gnome must trust that the Queen had made the right decision. And even if Mother gnome didn't know exactly what the little gnomes' task was, she was very proud that they were part of the plan.

Interpreter looked at them and said:

"This is no time for complaining. This is the best way to travel. Neither mylingar and ravens nor other witchcraft can spot us. But the dark makes it difficult for me to read the Queen's instructions."

His eyes smarted when he tried to make out the letters on the leather document.

"I am still your chosen cicerone meaning your guide. Chosen by the Queen and I have to be able to read the instructions. We should have a lantern carrier in here. If only the rucksack were a little bigger…" he mumbled to himself.

"Wait, I just remembered that I brought some gnome candles." Mother gnome fumbled in her little bag and hey presto, she had a gnome candle in her hand.

"You are so foresighted and wise, dear Mother gnome", said Father gnome and by the weak candle light you could see a smile on Father gnome's lips.

"Can you hold it a bit closer so I can read what it says?" muttered Interpreter who was pleased that the Mother gnome had brought the candles but he didn't want to praise her too much.

"What does it say? Can you read it out loud?" asked Sira eagerly.

She took hold of the string with both her hands as the rucksack shook. She wondered how she really could fit inside the rucksack but thought it was no use asking. She wouldn't get an answer anyway.

"I cannot reveal what it says. The Queen was very decisive on that. That I was not to tell…" It jolted again and Interpreter's head hit the inside but his fur-coated hand held tightly to the instructions. "As I was saying, I cannot reveal what it says here. Not yet. And I do not want you to ask or nag me about it. By the way, I will ask Skade where we are."

Interpreter folded the instructions and put them in his uniform pocket. He stroked his hand on his medal *For The Best Interpretation Ever* and smiled proudly.

With one hand gripping the string, he took hold of a seam and heaved himself upwards.

The rucksack bounced and he fell down. Interpreter tried to look free and easy and the others couldn't help giggling. He grabbed the string again and strong grip at seam and started to heave himself up again. Presently he fell down again. It jolted and jumped so much that they were all tossed about in the rucksack. Finally, they managed to sit up straight again and held steadily onto the strings.

"I think I will wait to ask Skade. We can trust that she finds the best way," he said and adjusted his fur cap and uniform with one hand. The others winked at each other. Skade was an unusually strong giantess. Cutting winds and sharp hailstones didn't bother her. She was well acquainted with the wilderness of Boreal and with long powerful strokes of her ski sticks, her skis whizzed forward on the blanket of snow. The lantern carrier did its job well and she didn't have to see where she was going. They had passed the valley surrounded by the five mountains and were half way into the woods which surrounded the Big lake. Skade knew that if they were going to win time she would have to take a short cut across the lake. The Big lake was very broad and wide and always covered with layers of ice. But it was treacherous because just when you thought the ice was thick and safe it could all of a sudden be thin and ready to burst. And then you'd be sucked down in the cold water and never reach the surface again. Skade was the only one who knew this and she wasn't going to tell the others, not even the lantern carrier which conveyed the light. To go around the lake wasn't an option.

When she had the lake in sight she slowed down and asked the lantern carrier to see if there was anywhere for them to stop. The lantern carrier swept around with its light and caught a clump of trees which would give them shelter.

"It seems we're stopping. Oh, how it tosses!" cried Father gnome and took hold of Mother gnome's hand. It felt like they'd fall from the sky and a great relief when they seemed to have landed on the ground. The rucksack opened and a big eye looked down on them and a dark voice said:

"Klixigt frugos? Skalgae habits."

"Skade asks if we are okay and says that we are having a break now," translated Interpreter and got on his feet.

Mother gnome hurried to take out some ancient water and everybody quaffed. And that was for the best because it wasn't good to be thirsty when you travelled. Fortunately, she also had bread for everyone. Father gnome smiled proudly at his wife and took a big bite.

While Skade and Interpreter talked silently, the others stretched their legs. Sira looked up at the ski sticks which stood leaning against a tree. She had never seen such long ski sticks not to mention the skis, as long as the football pitch back home. Beside the skis lay Skade's bow and koger. She tried to listen to what they were talking about but it was impossible to understand anything. The giant's language was far too complicated. The break didn't last long and Sira and the others held the strings tightly when Skade put on her rucksack.

"Skade says that we have to cross the lake. It can be a bit slippery but we have no choice if we are to gain time," Interpreter said and used his napkin to wipe off some sweet pearls from his forehead.

"We can do that. Just have to hold on," laughed Sira to cheer everybody up.

"Of course, we're going to make it," Mother gnome giggled and soon they were all laughing out loud.

Skade's skis sunk deeper into the snow when she approached the Big lake. She stopped by the edge for a while, took hold of the mountain on the other side which

Interpreter had pointed out to her. Skade took a deep breath and let her skis glide onto the ice which crunched under her weight. The lantern carrier expanded his light so she could see where it looked safe. With gigantic, powerful strokes of her ski sticks and long skis, Skade was soon in the middle of the lake. It was then it happened. A nasty cold crept around her.

"Hablit! Hablit!" she shouted and tried to stamp with her skis to warm up but an icy grip held them in deadlock. Skade looked down. The cold had twirled around her tall body and a groaning sound echoed in her ears. The lantern carrier on her shoulders almost fell off.

"What is it? Why are you stamping, Skade?" Interpreter asked as he poked his head out of the rucksack.

"You must carry the rucksack with care. We are tumbling around like snow balls here!" he continued.

Interpreter's irritation changed to fear when he saw Skade's face. He lowered himself down quickly and shouted:

"Ruvoj! It's Ruvoj! What are we going to do?"

Ruvoj was the most feared cold. It had carved long icy scratches in Skade's face and uttered a squeaking sound when it slowly but surely covered her with a layer of ice.

The cold found its way down the rucksack and slowly filled it with ice cubes. If nothing was done in an instant, they would soon be frozen in.

"What's happening? I'm cold. What is Ruvoj?" said Sira through chattering teeth. The others looked terrified. They knew that there wasn't much time left. Finally, Mother gnome started babbling a rhyme:

Dear cousins, please hear
All we feel is fear
Ruvoj has us in its grip
We can't move our hip
Help! Help! Help!

Skade was captured. The lantern carrier's light was out and the ice cubes filled the rucksack. Mother gnome didn't give up and continued saying the rhyme over and over again. The ice was up to their chins and even inside their ears. Everybody thought that this was their last moment and didn't hear the squeaking scream which came from the horrible cold when it had to let go of Skade and the rucksack. Slowly but surely the ice cubes began to melt and they heard Ruvoj's last squeaking scream before it was changed into happy voices.

Finally, Skade could move her arms and legs and she put down the lantern carrier which had begun to shine again. She brushed off the last icicles from her clothes and carefully took off the rucksack. Around her feet some small well-dressed characters danced.

"We made it! We made it! We're the best! No protest!" shouted the characters.

Skade opened the rucksack and Interpreter was the first to climb out. He looked somewhat disturbed as his uniform was a mess and his fur cap was askew as was his fine medal. After him came Sira, Father and Mother gnome. They were wet and cold.

"Hello there Father and Mother gnome! Long time no see. It's certainly a surprise to see you," exclaimed one of the well-dressed characters and strode forward to greet them.

"But how wet you are. You'd better follow us home to get dry and clean at once. Colds are no trifling matter in this climate," the character continued.

"Many thanks dear cousins. I'm so glad you heard me. We wouldn't have made it without you," said Mother gnome and tried to straighten her grey jacket and skirt. "We're very grateful. I don't think I've had the honour before…" Interpreter reached out his wet fur-clad glove which met a colourful mitten.

"We're spraettar. The gnomes' handsome cousins. Nice to meet you." The spraett laughed. Father gnome cleared his throat loudly.

"And who is this?" One of the other spraettar looked curiously at Sira, who reached out her hand.

"My name is Sira." The colourful and neat spraettar made her feel happy.

"And who is that? The one you can't see the head of?" The spraett looked up in the sky as possible. "And who is that who shines so bright?" continued the spraett.

"The tall one is Skade the giantess, who knows all about the wilderness of Boreal and the other one is a lantern carrier. I will ask them to wait here while we go with you," Interpreter said and made a sign to Skade to wait outside. She nodded, put down the lantern carrier and unstrapped her skis.

"Follow us," said the most talkative spraett and took the lead. The others followed in a line cross the ice to a small islet not far away. One of the spraettar knocked three times on a stone. The stone moved and they went down some steps. Below the stairs was an warm, lit room.

"Sit down here and warm yourselves and I'll get some hot drinks for you," said the spraett and hurried away.

They sat down on a carpet of fir twigs and felt the warmth filling their bodies. "The spraettar always have to be the best and the best looking. I don't understand how they can be when they live in a double bottomed lake and we live under a castle," muttered Father gnome.

"Come now, we don't have to be surly. If they hadn't come and rescued us, we wouldn't have made it. Cheer up!" said Mother gnome and patted Father gnome's cheek.

Sira thought that they really were alike but the spraettar had more colour and style than the gnomes.

Two of the spraettar came back with hot drinks which smelled of woods and humus.

"Drink this and you'll soon be on your feet again," one of them said.

Sira didn't like the taste but followed the spraett's advice.

"And what are you doing in the middle of the Big Lake? And at this hour when Ruvoj is most dangerous? You were lucky that we've the best of ears. But where are you heading?" said the spraett full of curiosity.

"We're on our way to El—" said Sira but was interrupted by Interpreter.

"We shall not mention any names. It can bring bad luck for those who are listening. I should say we are out on a mission," said Interpreter and fumbled in his uniform pocket, pulling out a wet leather document which he unfolded. He made a wry face. "Everything is erased! I cannot read the instructions!" No matter how hard he tried, the document was unreadable. The water in the rucksack had made the letters disappear.

"We'll make it anyway. We must have courage…" said Mother gnome and tried to calm him down.

A loud knock was heard from above.

"It must be Skade. We have to be on our way," Interpreter said. His voice turned to a whisper and his eyes filled with tears. Sira patted him on the shoulder.

"We'll make it," said Sira and got up. The most talkative spraett followed them to the stairs and said: "I just want to say how glad I am that we could be of help and I hope we'll see you again soon. Especially you, dear cousins, we don't see each other too often."

The spraett bowed. Father gnome felt a sting of bad conscience and bowed his head. They thanked the spraettar and went upstairs where Skade was ready. Interpreter said something in the giant's language and

Skade nodded whereafter Sira, Mother and Father gnome and Interpreter lowered themselves down inside the rucksack.

"Hold on tight. We are in a hurry. We have to be at the meeting point as soon as possible," said Interpreter as he straightened his medal and took a hold of the string. He fretted over the Queen's instructions being ruined and didn't know how to solve the problem.

Skade set off at full speed on her skis with the lantern carrier on her shoulders. Mother and Father gnome sat close to each other.

Sira wrapped the string around her wrist and if as she had read Interpreter's mind she said, "What are we going to do about the instructions? If we can't follow them, we can't catch El—"

"Don't mention her name. Like I said before, mentioning her name can mean bad luck," Interpreter said harshly. Sira avoided his gaze. It jumped and bumped inside the rucksack and they could hear the frizzling noise of Skade's skis.

"We must hope that we don't run into any more problems before we reach the meeting point. Then maybe all is for nothing," said Mother gnome. She held tightly to Father gnome's hand so that he wouldn't fall over her.

"What about the instructions?" Sira tried again.

"I am thinking. Please do not disturb me," said Interpreter. He closed his eyes and pursed his thin lips.

Mother gnome looked at Sira and rolled her peppercorn eyes. Sira tried not to laugh.

The sleigh ride and Guolldo

A while after Skade had left the castle, the stars moved from the east. Two falor dressed in long black coats with broad glittering waist belts stepped out from the castle. They had fur hats and long black plaits with feathers hung down their backs. Their reindeer-skinned boots didn't leave any footprints in the snow as they walked towards the sleighs.

The falor were protectors and as such they had the direct order of the Queen to transport a sleigh each to Elakka's hiding place. Their black-painted eyes beamed in green and blue when they saw that everybody was in place. Four lantern carriers and six little gnomes in one sleigh and four lantern carriers, the little gnome Nol and the dwarves Moltas and Elle in the other.

Cloven feet stamped and reindeer horns scraped against each other when the falor seated themselves in the sleighs. Calls and lashes, the front reindeers set off closely followed by the other reindeers and the avenue soon turned into an open landscape. In the light of the lantern carriers you could see how swarms of snowflakes were thrown here and there in the icy wind, desperately trying to penetrate the little passengers' reindeer rugs. Ice patches hid below the new snow. The sleighs skidded forwards and backwards but the reindeers responded to the falor's every hint and shortly they travelled steadily forward. The Queen had also sent her best peregrines which guided them from the air with their loud *"Ke-ke-ke"*.

After some time, the landscape changed: steep mountains loomed large and the way disappeared in deep snow which forced the reindeers to fight forward. The falor urged them on but their voices and the whip's lashing sound disappeared in the gale as they slowed down.

Snowflakes covered the sleighs and the passengers hid under the rugs. The reindeers panted; the heat from their bodies steamed as they struggled forward in the snow. The falor continued to urge them on and when their energy faltered, the pilgrims led them into a valley. The gale continued and piles of snow built up but here and there the ground was hard. The falor roared and whip lashes whined through the air. The reindeers started galloping and sleighs flew forward.

"Ke-ke-ke!"

They turned right, into a smaller valley. The mountaintops were higher and the wind subsided. The peregrines sailed downwards. The falor pulled the reins and the reindeers slowed down; the birds landed close to some stone blocks. It was time to rest.

The lantern carriers jumped out of the sleighs and grouped themselves to light up the dark. The little gnomes crawled out of the rugs. They were both hungry and thirsty after the long trip and were lifted out of the sleighs. While the food was taken out and the fire made ready, they helped one of the falor to feed the reindeers, which scraped impatiently with their hooves. They calmed down when the little hands gave them reindeer moss to eat. The peregrines were also fed. They sat at a safe distance and fought over the raw meat which was thrown at them. The little gnomes stood closely together and watched with big peppercorn eyes when the sharp beaks grabbed and pulled the pieces of meat.

The two dwarves, Moltas and his sister Elle, were very handy and were responsible for everything practical. They fetched spruce twigs and some logs of wood from the sleighs and soon everybody was seated around the warming fire. The little gnomes sat closely together and their eyes followed the crackling sparks whirling up in the sky. The lantern carriers turned down their lights and rested. Lukewarm spruce shoots, bread and a strengthening drink put everybody in a good mood.

"Please Moltas, can't you tell us a story?" asked Elle and drank down the hot drink noisily.

"I don't know if I can," said Moltas. He was hungry and took a bite of the bread.

"Please, please, Moltas!" pleaded the little gnomes.

"You can tell the story of the lynx's ear tuft. It's so exciting!" said Elle with beaming eyes.

"What? The lynx's ear tuft?" said Nol, surprised. Nol could talk to the animals so he sharpened his ears. "What kind of story is that? I want to hear it!"

"But I've already told it once," said Moltas and fumbled in his pocket.

"But it was only to us at the dinner", said Elle. When you were late…"

"We haven't heard it and we want to hear it," said one of the little gnomes firmly.

"Okay then. I can tell it again." Moltas took up the ear tuft from his pocket and held it up towards the firelight. The eyes of the falor glowed.

"What? Is it a real ear tuft? Where did you get it from?" said Nol and almost fell backwards.

"It happened when I sat myself on a stone to see the fireworks in the sky better. That's why I was late for the dinner. I noticed that I was sitting on a lynx and I happened to hold its ear and then—" Moltas was interrupted by sharp *"Ke-ke-ke"* which cut through the air and the peregrines dived down towards the circle around the fire.

They flapped their wings and their worried sounds made the party realise that they had to leave. Within minutes Moltas had put out the fire and the lantern carriers seated themselves in the sleighs and put on their lights at full strength.

Nol sat beside Moltas and hoped to hold the ear tuft at least once.

"We'd better buckle up. It might be a trip we'd soon rather forget," said one of the falor while she put a rope around the little gnomes' rug. And the others did what she said.

"Ke-ke-ke!" The peregrines hung poised in the air.

It didn't snow but the wind increased and a storm was coming their way. The falor howled, lashes shot through the air. The front reindeers put on a burst of speed. The sleighs set out over the hard snow guided by the peregrines. Rumbling sounds were heard from the high mountaintops far away. The little gnomes held hands tightly under the rug.

The cries of the peregrines lead them into a narrow passage. The reindeers plunged forward. The mountain walls came surprisingly near when the ground beneath the sleighs became uneven and angular, the wind was strong. The falor pulled the reins and the reindeers slowed down. Steam rose from their bodies and their breathing was heavy. One of the peregrines dropped fast and landed on the right shoulder of one of the falor. It pecked lightly on the fala's cheek with its slightly bent, sharp beak.

"What is it?" asked the fala and pushed back her fur cap from her ear and waited for the bird's words. It pecked on her cheek again.

"What do you want to tell me?" said the fala urgently.

The peregrine pointed with its wing towards the mountaintops. They were covered with dark clouds and hard to see. The fala's eyes followed the bird's pointed wing and saw what it meant.

"Guolldo!" The peregrine answered by lifting from her shoulder and flying in front of the first reindeer.

"Guolldo!" shouted the fala.

Her voice travelled like fire through sleighs and bodies. Everybody was struck by fear.

The fala made the whip lash through the air. The front reindeer took off at a gallop, followed by the reindeers behind. The peregrines formed a flying circle around the sleighs and tried to keep them together with the help of their cries.

The feared snowstorm Guolldo had risen. Something had brought him out of his deep sleep. Something that flapped and shouted around his head. Irritated, he stretched his body and it howled and roared even more. When his big mouth gasped the whirls of snow rumbled and his breath formed large snowdrifts.

The fala pulled the reins, turned around and saw the other sleigh right behind. The peregrines landed on the sleighs and the fala shouted: "We must get past him! Stay together! Follow me!"

Three of the birds lifted and formed around the sleighs to help them stay together. The fourth sat on the fala's shoulder to help her steer the sleigh. The lantern carriers struggled to lighten up the way in front of them. The poor visibility made it hard to see the large snowdrifts.

Guolldo had opened his big eyes. The flapping, cawing and shouting made him extremely annoyed. The mountaintops cracked when he turned his head but he still couldn't figure out where the noise came from. When he saw the sleighs at the bottom of the valley, he reached out his long arms and tried to catch them with his bloated hands. The sleighs lifted and fell flat again. Guolldo's angry voice resounded in the valley and built high snow walls and thick drifts. He tried again and again. When the sleighs lifted and fell flat for the fourth time, they flew in different directions and he lost sight of them. He fought with his arms and his angry roars started avalanches which rumbled down the steep mountainsides. Huge masses of snow hurried down the long valley towards the little characters in the sleighs. It flapped and cawed around Guolldo's head but instead of the roars there was scornful laughter. Spiteful laughter.

Guolldo waved his arm tiredly and fell asleep in a wink. The only thing you could hear was his deep snores which echoed in the mountaintops.

The sleigh was upside down; the snow was still falling heavily. Weak lights lay scattered in the snow. The fala stood up and hurried to the sleigh. She was relieved when she saw that everybody was safe. Moltas touched his head. He had a big bump but both Elle and Nol seemed to be safe. The fala picked up the lantern carriers which were half buried in the snow. The reindeers stood gathered around some trees a bit away. The fala looked but couldn't see the other sleigh.

"Where did she go?" asked Elle bewildered.

"Who do you mean?" Moltas turned around.

"The fala, of course. She was here just now and now she's gone!" said Elle.

"I can't see her either. How strange," said Nol and put his cap straight.

"She can't leave us like that, can she? We don't know where we're going, do we? And where's the other sleigh with the little gnomes in? By the way, I'm freezing." Elle shivered.

"Come Elle, let's go to the reindeers. We can look for some sticks and light a fire. Nol, you come too. And you too, lantern carriers. Shine your lights so we can see," said Moltas.

The lantern carriers took the lead closely followed by Moltas and the others. Elle placed herself between two reindeers to get some warmth. The lantern carriers shone their lights hither and thither so that Moltas and Nol could find some sticks.

"I hope that nothing has happened to my siblings. Mother and Father would never forgive the Queen if anything happened to them," said Nol and bent down to pick up a couple of sticks.

"We really must hope that nothing has happened. The fala has probably gone to look for them. I'm sure she'll be back soon," said Moltas, trying to sound calm.

A bit further off one of the lantern carriers' lights began to blink. Nol and Moltas hurried to see what it was.

"One of the peregrines!" said Nol desperately and crouched beside the peregrine in the snow.

"Is it dead?" said Moltas and crouched.

"No, but it's very weak." Nol stroked the peregrine.

"What's happened? Oh no! Poor peregrine. Is it alive?" Elle got tears in her eyes.

"It's a little alive. But what's this?" said Nol. His hand fumbled over something on the peregrine's wing. It twitched. One of the lantern carriers shone some extra light.

"A spear! A spear! Someone has shot the Queen's peregrine! Poor you," said Nol compassionately and patted the peregrine carefully.

"Can I see?" Moltas bent over the peregrine. "Just as I thought. There are only some that have this kind of spear. The point has a barb which is very difficult to remove. And it contains a poison as well. The peregrine probably hasn't much time left." Moltas looked very worried.

"There must be something we can do!" said Elle and stroked its beak.

"What do you mean? Who are they who have this kind of a spear? Is it true that we can't save it?" said Nol with tears streaming down his cheeks.

"We can't save it. It's Elakka's spies' doings. They have spears like this. The horrible mylingar and their even more horrible ravens that they fly around on," said Moltas sadly.

It whistled above their heads. The lantern carrier turned off their lights and everybody huddled up.

"What's happened here?" asked the fala, who had since reappeared. She spoke in a dark tone.

"Was it you... Such a blessing. We thought it was mylingar," said Elle with a sigh of relief.

She straightened herself. The lantern carriers hurried to turn on their lights and pointed it towards the peregrine.

"It has been shot," sobbed Nol and gently stroked the visibly lifeless peregrine.

"A spear. I know who makes them and it's not us dwarves. The point has a barb which contains poison and—" said Moltas and fell silent when the fala interrupted him.

"Let me have a look." The fala crouched and put her hand on the peregrine. "It's very weak and it mustn't die. Can you move?"

The fala took off her gloves and the others stepped back. The fala started mumbling in an incomprehensible language and put her hand across the wound where the spear was stuck. A strong light bored its way around the spear point which loosened. Moltas hurried to remove it. The fala took one of her leather bags from the sparkling belt. She poured out a strong scented powder mixture in one hand which made them wrinkle their noses. The fala mumbled a string of words three times while she put the powder around the bird and on the wound:

Roots, claws, meat
Give this bird feet
Feathers, bones, rings
Give this bird wings.

The fala went quiet and everybody looked anxiously at the bird which laid motionless with closed eyes. After a while, it opened its beak and a low *"ke-ke-ke"* was heard. It opened its eyes and was on its feet in an instant, flapping its wings. Nol jumped up and down with joy and laughed.

"It's alive! It made it! Thank you fala, thank you!" he shouted out loud.

The fala looked at him with a rare smile on her face. The peregrine lifted from the ground and disappeared with a loud *"Ke-ke-ke"*. Moltas studied the poisonous spear closely and then he buried it deep in the snow. The fala's forehead wrinkled as she thought, then she said:

"It was most probably mylingar on their ravens who woke Guolldo from his deep sleep. Luckily, the peregrine survived."

"But I wonder where the other sleigh is. Where are the little gnomes? Are they in trouble?" said Elle and looked at the fala while Nol asked:

"Where are my siblings?"

The fala turned to Nol.

"They're not in any danger. They are not too far from here. The sleigh had tipped over but none of them were hurt. The other fala and the little gnome awaits us there. We must hurry to them so we'll be in time at the meeting point.

"Don't you falas have any names? Are you really only called falor? How did you do that with the light on the peregrine? Did it really come from your hands?" asked Elle and climbed into the sleigh.

Moltas and Nol looked curiously at the fala when they fastened themselves.

"Don't ask so much, Elle," said the fala and tightened her cap on her head. The fala urged the reindeers which rushed off with the lantern carriers' light in front of them. The peregrines kept a watchful eye on them from the sky.

The leprechauns

The sulky leprechauns had to wait at the castle until Skade and the falor were gone. The Queen didn't trust them. She had heard about their pranks and mischief during dinner and now they were being sent home before anything else could happen.

Outside the gates a sleigh waited and most reluctantly they jumped into it. After a signal from the guards that all eight were there, the reindeers set off. But the leprechauns' surly looks didn't last long. In the shadows of the fire torches on the side of the sleigh, you could see eager movements. The muffled sound of hooves and the hissing slides in the snow hid the foolish pranks they got up to.

The winding way led them across open landscapes. Some snowflakes danced in the cold wind. After a few miles they turned into the woods, the snow became deeper and deeper and the five reindeers had to work harder to move forward. Soon they were surrounded by tall, old trees. They swayed slowly and their creaking sound sang a lullaby.

The leprechauns went quiet. They loved lullabies and they leaned back and closed their eyes. A snow owl flew over them, the snow from its wings fell on leprechauns' faces like a powder but none of them noticed it.

They didn't know how long they'd been asleep when they were suddenly awoken by a crackling sound. The front reindeer bellowed and backed up. A couple of reindeers pulled and jerked the reins. One leprechaun jumped forward and grabbed hold of the reins to try to calm them down.

The crackling sound was heard again. It sounded like sparkles from a fire but they couldn't tell where it came from. The reindeers moved forward and soon one of the leprechauns pointed at a green and blue whining light which closed up from behind. Fear took hold of them. They whistled and waved with their napkins trying hard to make the light go away. But instead it shone even brighter and the crackling sound came closer. The reindeers ran forward and suddenly they were treading on thin ice. The sleigh went here and there and the reindeers' couldn't get a grip. Green, blue and white light phenomena danced around them and the crackling noise whined in their pointy ears. Fire foxes! It was their tails which danced around them.

The leprechauns huddled up together. They knew that when the fire foxes' tails showed themselves it was best to hold on to their cocked hats because if you were hatless they could burn your hair. And none of them wanted their red hair to become ashes.

The tails got closer and closer to the sleigh. The leprechauns thought that this was Mother gnome's way of punishing them for playing pranks at the dinner. They promised each other, solemnly, that if only the fire foxes would take their tails and disappear, they would never tease the gnomes again, ever. In the midst of that thought something unexpected happened. Lots of balls of yarn came rolling. It flashed and banged as they attacked the fire foxes from every angle. The reindeers came to a halt. The leprechauns couldn't believe their eyes. The fire foxes did everything to get away but the balls of yarn were everywhere. They tied themselves around the foxes' tails; the foxes desperately tried to get away by wriggling hither and thither.

More and more balls of yarn came rolling and the crackling sound got weaker and weaker. And then it stopped and it became dark. The only thing you could hear was the reindeers' puffing and grunting.

The fire torches on the sledge had gone out and leprechauns couldn't see anything. They thought that their last moment had come. The balls of yarn would surely eat them. Oh, how they regretted playing pranks at the dinner!

It scraped and scratched around the sleigh and they almost got tears in their eyes. But instead of being attacked it lit up on all sides and the most beautiful being they'd ever seen stood by them. The leprechauns couldn't be anything but taken aback but they soon collected their wits and took off their cocked hats and bowed their wrinkled heads.

"Leprechauns, you do not have to take off your hats for my sake," said the being with a calm and confident voice.

The leprechauns put on their hats and couldn't take their eyes off the being standing in front of them. She wore a grey dress and the wind played with her long blond hair. Her eyes shifted from green to blue and the mouth showed a smile.

"Lucky you that I was close by. You cannot trifle with fire foxes," said the being and put the last ball of yarn together with the rest in the basket beside her.

"I do not know what you did to get them to come after you. I have not seen them so upset in a long time. You must know that you cannot whistle, swear or wave with your napkins when they are about? If you do, it will not end well," said the being and frowned.

The leprechauns looked down in shame. It was exactly what they had done, whistled and waved with their napkins. But they hadn't sworn at all. They thought themselves very lucky to have been saved by the being and her balls of yarn.

"I think you have learned your lesson well. Let us forget about it. You can follow me home and have something to eat. You must be very hungry after all the adventure. I have food and water for your reindeers too. They must need it. Where are you going by the way?" said the being when it smiled at them and set off in the direction of a couple of mountains. The balls of yarn groused in the basket. The reindeers followed happily with firm steps and the leprechauns sat quietly and almost enchanted. They didn't dare to say that they were on their way home as they had been in trouble at the Queen's party. Large snowflakes fell slowly from the sky. The being began to sing a lullaby and the leprechauns felt how tired they were after everything that had happened and totally unsuspecting, they fell asleep one by one in the sleigh.

The miner's wife

Is it time to wake up now sleepyheads. You've been sleeping far too long," said a harsh voice.

The leprechauns looked around drowsily. It was pitch-black and smelled somewhat stale. The sleigh and the soft skin rugs were gone. Instead they were lying on something hard and damp. Fear crept along their spines. They sat up quickly and groped for each other's hands. A pair of shining green blue eyes stared at them.

"I see you but you can't see me. Hahaha!"

The leprechauns were more than frightened. They thought the voice sounded like the being but much harder.

"Actually, I don't like visitors. But when I saw how you waved with your napkins and whistled at the fire foxes I couldn't help but catch you. It's one of the worst things I know, to wave and whistle. Besides, I know that you can get three wishes if you catch a leprechaun and you're many more…" The voice chuckled.

Some fire torches lit up. The leprechauns huddled up even closer when they saw that they were in some kind of a cave. And they panicked when they realised that they were locked up in a cage with a big lock. There seemed to be no way out. The being crouched in front of the cage.

"You're so gullible. Did you think I was kind and beautiful, that my voice was soft and nice?"

The being moved her hand across the grousing balls of yarn which lay in the basket beside her. Her face wasn't very kind and beautiful any more and her eyes were black.

The leprechauns' eyes filled with tears which slowly ran down their wrinkled faces. Mother gnome couldn't be so mean as to send them here for their mischief, could she?

The being stood up and its grey dress swept over the cage. The long blonde hair was put up in a knot which was full of spider webs and dead flies.

"I'll give you something to eat. Just as I promised." The balls of yarn rushed out of the basket.

"No, not you. It's the leprechauns who are having something to eat now. You have to wait," shouted the being and pointed towards the basket.

The balls of yarn rolled back quickly. They squeaked and groused. One of them stopped in front of the cage and stared at the leprechauns with its horrific little eyes. For eyes it had and now the leprechauns could see that it wasn't just an ordinary ball of yarn which they had thought at the beginning. No, this was wound wool and pieces of cloth with old hair, broken nails and other disgusting things stuck to it. The leprechauns looked at it terrified to the bones and gave a jump when it opened its mouth and a long thin black tongue with small warts shot through the bars. The being kicked the ball of yarn and it landed squeaking in the basket.

"Don't scare the little leprechauns. You'll have yours later."

The being took out a key made of shiny silver. The leprechauns loved everything that shone and couldn't take their eyes off it. But as soon as the key was put in the key hole, they felt scared again.

"You must eat and drink properly. I've a mission for you later." The being pushed a tray through the cage door and then locked it.

The leprechauns didn't know that they had been tricked and caught by the miner's wife. The miner's wife lived by the foot of a mountain and preferred solitude in darkness. She'd one craving and that was to find gold, silver and other valuable things deep inside caves and mountains. To help her find it, she had a treasure compass with a needle made of silver. To get the gold which the compass pointed out to her she always sent out her handmade disgusting balls of yarn.

Now the treasure compass pointed in the direction of a mountain where there were lots of emeralds, diamonds and other gleaming gems. But the way into the mountain was too narrow and complicated, which made the miner's wife very angry. Neither she nor the balls of yarn could get to the treasure but now she'd the chance to get it.

She looked towards the cage where the frightened leprechauns sat in a corner. Their wrinkled hands would soon have a task she thought and laughed spitefully to herself.

"Well, well my dear leprechaun, the time's come for you to help me," said the miner's wife and crouched before the cage. "I'm going to unlock the door now and I want you to come out and stand here before me. Don't you dare consider running away," she continued.

As soon as the leprechauns stepped out of the cage, the balls of yarn rolled out of the basket and surrounded them with their squeaking and grousing. The leprechauns held each other's hands tightly and didn't dare to do anything but stand absolutely still with their cocked hats on the sides. They wondered what it was that they were going to help it with but none of them dared to ask.

"There's a sledge outside. It'll take you to a mountain. Inside that mountain there's something that I want and you're going to get it for me," said the miner's wife unkindly. The leprechauns didn't dare to do anything but nod in assent. They thought this was for the best because otherwise terrible things could happen.

She picked up the basket and the balls of yarn jumped into the sleigh. For once they were completely silent. But leprechauns felt how the balls glared at them and some of them put out their warty tongues out to them. The miner's wife gave the leprechauns a pat with her knotty staff, so that the snake head at the top swayed.

"Now, now get out of the cave and into the sleigh. You'll sit in the front and I'll sit in the back so I can keep an eye on you. Don't do anything stupid," she said and clicked her tongue.

The leprechauns got in the sleigh. They shivered from head to toe when they saw that there were three black reindeers strapped to it and they were afraid just to think about what task she'd in mind for them. The miner's wife lashed her whip and the black reindeers set full speed ahead across snow and ice. The leprechauns clung to the sides so as not to fall out. They thought that they'd never come home again.

For the leprechauns it felt like an eternity before the miner's wife finally slowed the reindeers down. She made them stop at some sculpture-like snow piles. She got out of the sleigh and looked up on the black mountain top before them.

"Here it is. Somewhere inside that mountain is the treasure." The miner's wife laughed scornfully and turned to the leprechauns. "Now we'll see what you're made of. You've strong arms I hope. Hahaha!"

The meeting point

In a valley by the foot of a mountain, where the woods gave temporary shelter against snow and ice, they gathered around a fire in front of a windshield. The reindeers stood in a bunch and ate lichen. The peregrines were nowhere to be seen and the lantern carriers' lights were out.

Skade had taken off her skis which leaned against the tallest tree along with the ski sticks. The arrows and the koger laid at the foot of the trunk. She sat with her legs crossed a bit further from the others and rocked the little gnomes, wrapped up in fur. They'd been over the moon when they saw their parents. Now they were tired after a trip full of hardships and almost asleep.

And that was for the best as what was being discussed wasn't for small ears. Each and every one told, in a low voice, about their experiences since they left the castle and they all agreed that it must have been Elakka who had used her dark powers to try to stop them. Interpreter spoke:

"Her spies are everywhere. We must be careful. Even if mylingar and their ravens are loud and noisy, they can also be almost soundless."

One of the falor got on her feet.

"And their spears are so poisonous that they could kill us," added Moltas.

Everybody shuddered and huddled up at the thought of mylingar and their dangerous spears.

"Not to talk about other dangers Elakka could have let loose. We'd better keep watch while you go through what should be done," said the fala.

The other fala stood up. Sira gave Interpreter a slight push to the side and looked at him.

"Hrm, hrm. Before you leave there's one thing I have to say," Interpreter said and stood up and straightened his uniform.

"I... hrm-hrm, I..."

"Get to the point. We've to go," said the fala, irritated.

"The instructions... the instructions are ruined. They are unreadable. It happened when Ruvoj attacked us on the Big lake. They became all wet."

Interpreter took out the wrinkled leather document from his uniform pocket. He fidgeted about. Sira, Mother and Father gnome looked down prepared for the others comments. But it went quiet.

After a while, the other fala said worriedly:

"It's a problem. Without the Queen's instructions we can't find the entrance to Elakka's hideout or know how to catch her."

Interpreter didn't know where to look. The Queen had given him the instructions in greatest confidence and he had failed. He, Interpreter, who had received a medal for *The Best Interpretation Ever.* He was not worthy of it any more. He sat down and hung his head. Sira put her arm around him.

"It's not your fault that the instructions became wet and unreadable. How could we know that Ruvoj was on its hunt when we crossed the Big lake?"

"It's not your fault," said Mother and Father gnome at the same time.

"We don't think so either." Moltas and Elle looked encouragingly at Interpreter and Nol agreed:

"It's really not your fault. It could have happened to any of us."

Interpreter felt a bit better at heart. One of the falor took up a small reed and blew lightly in it.

And it didn't take long before the peregrines came sailing through the air. They landed close to the falor who crouched, stroked their feathers and whispered something to them. Shortly both the falor and the peregrines were gone.

"That's exactly what happened when the sleigh overturned, isn't it?" shouted Elle, terrified. "First, the fala was there and next she wasn't. Now both are gone! What are we going to do now? What if mylingar comes? What if…"

"Calm down, Elle. So far so good. She came back, didn't she? She saved the peregrine," said Moltas soothingly.

"Do not forget that the falor are protectors. But they are also shape-shifters. My interpretation is that they have left to get help," said Interpreter and sneezed. "You're not catching a cold, are you?" asked Mother gnome. She picked up a tissue from her bag and gave it to him. Interpreter took it gratefully and blew his nose carefully.

"I hope they'll be back soon," said Sira nervously.

The falor had disappeared without saying anything. Suddenly she came to think of her grandmother. During the whole trip she'd forgotten that she really was a human and that she now was in… Yes, where *was* she? In some kind of fairy-tale world? She should be at her nan's, lying on the blue couch listening to her stories. What if all imagination disappeared. Every story. Then everything fun in life would die.

Sira buried her head in her hands. Tears poured down her cheeks.

"Oh dearest. What's the matter?" said Mother gnome and squeezed herself in between Interpreter and Sira.

"Don't cry. Do you hear? Here's a tissue. Dry your eyes and tell me what it is," said Mother gnome in a calm voice. Sira dried her eyes but the tears kept running down her cheeks.

"I miss my grandmother. Mum doesn't care. Since they divorced she's changed. She just works all the time. And if imagination disappears my grandmother will also change," sobbed Sira.

"Come, come Sira. It's not too late," Mother gnome consoled and continued: "We're here to help each other and…"

As if from nowhere, the falor appeared.

"Where did you go?" asked Elle, annoyed. "Why do you disappear without saying anything? What would we've done if mylingarna came? What—"

"You ask too many questions, Elle," said the fala and held out a leather document to Interpreter.

"Here are the instructions again. The Queen asked us to tell you it's urgent. She'd received word that Elakka knows that we're coming for her and we must find her hideout before it's too late. She also said that she trusts you, Interpreter and that you, Sira must hold out. You're the key in all this." Fala's blue green eyes turned to Sira. "You mustn't give up hope," she said and then the two falor went to stand guard.

Sira wanted to believe the fala's words. She looked around and there was everybody who had fought so hard to get here. They'd become her friends and they were prepared to give everything to stop Elakka. She must believe in the fala's words. And if she was the key, she, Sira, wouldn't give up hope. And she must believe that imagination would survive. Interpreter unfolded the instructions.

"Aren't you reading them out loud?" asked Nol, disappointed.

"This will take some time," said Interpreter and turned to the lantern carriers. "Lantern carriers, follow me and give me some light so I can read what is written. The rest of you have to wait a while. I must go through this in peace and quiet."

The lynx

The fire crackled. The trees sighed around them. Skade sat leaning against some tree trunks and slept deeply with the little gnomes in her arms. Mother and Father gnome almost fell down with fatigue.

"Maybe I can have a look at that ear tuft now?" asked Nol with an excited look at Moltas.

"I also want to see what it looks like," said Sira curiously. "I've only seen a lynx in a picture before. No, I saw a lynx when we went to the zoo a few years ago. But it was so far away that you could hardly see it."

Nol, Moltas and Elle looked bewildered. They had no idea what she was talking about. Seen in a picture and at a zoo? She must come from a strange place, the human. Moltas picked up the ear tuft from his pocket. In the firelight it looked like a bunch of black hair in his clenched fist.

"Is it really an ear tuft? From a lynx?" asked Nol.

"Yes it is. Look, the hairs are fixed here," answered Moltas and opened his hand to show them. At that moment, the wind took it.

"No, no! It's blowing away! Hurry up and catch it!" shouted Moltas.

Nol jumped up and down trying to catch it with his little hands. But the ear tuft didn't want to be caught and sailed away amongst the trees. Elle, who had a practical mind, rushed to light a fire torch which she quickly gave to Nol.

"Hurry Nol! You mustn't let it get out of your sight."

Nol grabbed the fire torch and ran after the ear tuft which was disappearing from the firelight and flew even further in amongst the trees. Nol's short legs had never run so fast. He shone with the fire torch here and there so as not to lose sight of the it.

Suddenly it was gone. Nol stopped and used the fire torch to look around. Where could it have gone? He went a bit further, towards some bushes and there, there it was. It was stuck on a twig.

Nol reached out his hand to grab it and was just about to take it when a weak screaming sound was heard. He turned around and saw a pair of yellowish eyes staring at him from a short distance away. He recognised the sound. It was a lynx and it was closing in on him. He knew that lynxes could be very dangerous, especially for little gnomes, if you happened to call it by its real name. It was then he remembered the string of words and the words poured out of his mouth:

"Goepan, Goepan, Goepan
You mustn't be mad.
Or I will turn into wolf,
And that will be very sad."

But the lynx continued to scream and came even closer. Nol didn't dare to move but he raised his voice and showed his teeth.

"Goepan, Goepan, Goepan
You mustn't be mad.
Or I will turn into wolf,
And that will be very sad."

The lynx was now so close that he could feel its breath. Nol shivered. He hadn't called the lynx by its real name. He'd said 'Goepan'. And he was sure that he'd shown his teeth. What if it didn't help? Then he would be eaten in a flash.

The lynx bent his head so that the ear was in front of Nol's face. Nol shone with the fire torch and saw that its ear tuft was missing. The one he was holding in his hand. Of course! It wanted its ear tuft back.

Nol put the fire torch in the snow and used both his hands to put the ear tuft back on its ear. The lynx gave him a friendly push which made Nol fall backwards in the snow. He laughed, stood up, brushed off the snow and patted the lynx. It bent down and whispered something in Nol's ear and disappeared amongst the trees.

Nol gasped. He couldn't believe that it was true that he'd come so close to a lynx and that it had whispered a secret in his ear.

"What took you so long? Did you get hold of the ear tuft?" said Elle and could hardly contain herself.

"Yes, we thought you might have been eaten," said Moltas and looked sanctimoniously at Elle.

Nol sat down by the fire and told them:

"Yes, I found it… and the lynx that had lost it…" he said secretively.

"What! What are you saying? Did you find the lynx that I took the ear tuft from?" said Moltas nervously.

"Yes, or more like it found me," said Nol and smiled.

"Weren't you terrified it might eat you?" said Elle and bit her nails.

"Yes, first I was really scared and thought that it would swallow me in one go but then it only wanted its ear tuft back," said Nol proudly.

"Did it get it back?" asked Sira and looked at Nol with big eyes.

"Yes, and I got to pat it!" said Nol even prouder.

"Is that true? Did you really pat it?" Elle's eyes were now bigger than Sira's. Nol looked dreamingly into the fire.

"I got to pat it and it whispered a secret to me."

"What's the secret? Say! Say!" said Elle and jumped up and down in front of the fire.

"I can't. It's a secret. Maybe you'll know later…" said Nol and winked at Elle.

"Everybody, listen up," said Interpreter and stepped towards the fire. Mother and Father gnome sat up drowsily. Skade moved and the little gnomes peeked out of the rug. Sira, Moltas, Elle and Nol looked excited.

"The falor? Where are the falor? And the peregrines? We must begin now," said Interpreter indignantly.

"We're here."

The falor, in their long black coats, came as usual out of nowhere. And the peregrines landed by their sides.

"We've searched the area and we haven't discovered anything suspicious so far. But we can't be too sure. It's best if we're as quiet as possible," said one fala and glanced at the other.

"You never know with Elakka. That is why we have to hurry. I have read the instructions very carefully", said Interpreter and struck his hand across his medal. "This is what we are going to do…" Everybody huddled up in a circle around Interpreter. Skade bent her tall body and turned her ear towards them.

"Sira, your task will be…" whispered Interpreter.

A low mumbling was heard. After some time they put out the fire and left for Elakka's den. Skade went ahead to stop any danger that might lie in waiting. No one, not even a bear would dare to set about her. Skade who was taller than the tallest and very, very strong.

The castle

At the castle, the atmosphere was everything but high spirited. The Queen paced back and forth. The Illustrious made deep scratches in the round table. The Powerful swung its knotty branches and the Ethereal spat and hissed.

You could still only see dim frost sculptures in the crystal ball on the table. It was impossible to make it show something else. Maybe Elakka had destroyed it or was it mylingar and the ravens when they banged and shouted inside it? It was impossible to know.

The Queen and the others around the table had been alarmed when the falor came back to get new instructions. They had told her what Ruvoj and Guolldo had done. She was grateful that everybody had made it but dreaded what Elakka might do next.

To stop Elakka was out of her power as the Queen didn't have any ties to her. When she, a long time ago expelled her from Boreal by chaining her deep inside a mountain, Elakka cut off the ties between them. And the Queen could therefore never lay a hand on Elakka ever. She had to put all her hopes on her inhabitants and Sira.

The heavenly spectacle of Aurora Borealis and the constellation of the Lynx, the Queen saw as a sign of possible defeat and the return of imagination. But considering everything that had happened, the Queen felt great concern. She couldn't understand how Elakka had managed to set herself free and get out of the mountain. Maybe Elakka was stronger and more evil than she'd believed earlier?

The falor had also said that the Lynx hadn't shown itself to them at any time, which made the Queen even more worried. The lynx was the guardian of all lost magical knowledge and she knew that when the constellation of the Lynx showed itself in the sky, its black ear tufts changed into antennas. Antennas which could take in all magical information about the lost knowledge. But now, neither Sira nor any of the inhabitants had met the lynx... And the new instructions she gave to the falor were only taken from her memory. What if she'd forgotten something?

"If they don't manage to destroy Elakka, what will happen to us?" said the Illustrious and hung its head.

"Nobody knows," said the Powerful and dropped some old leaves on the floor.

"And what about us? We who are invisible? What will happen to us?" said the Ethereal who hadn't said anything the whole time and began to get weak contours.

"We're here because we are the most powerful in Boreal," said the Queen.

"As leaders we must stand strong even if it is out of our control whether Elakka is destroyed or not. If we give up hope, Elakka has won. We must hold on and put our faith in their success. Elakka weakened us when she cut the ties with me but nothing is lost yet."

The preparations

Despite the fact that Skade had gone ahead to secure the way, they were very careful when they left for Elakka's den. Moltas and Elle had covered both sleighs and the reindeers hooves with a fabric that protected them from the sounds of squeaking snow. At the back of the sleighs hung track hiders which covered their tracks that would otherwise reveal their route. Trees and bushes along the way helped them and didn't drop a single snowflake that could reveal their whereabouts.

The peregrines sat on the lantern carriers' shoulders so they wouldn't be detected in the air. The lantern carriers had their weakest non-traceable lights on, so that the falor could steer the reindeers right. The little gnomes sat perfectly silent together with their parents in one of the sleighs. Mother gnome had knitted them a cap each. With the help of Boreal's famous Spider mother, she'd weaved in magical stitches that would protect the little gnomes from danger.

In the other sleigh it was also perfectly silent. No one dared utter a single word or even a hawking that could reveal their whereabouts. The falor steered the reindeers with safe hands and soon they spotted Elakka's den which distinguished itself in the winter landscape from a long distance.

The mountain top was snowless and almost black. When they got closer they saw that the mountain sides were all brown. Nothing grew there. If you would try to climb up along the sides, sharp ice tongues would get hold of you and drag you down into big sinkholes, and you'd never come up again. So it was best to take another way.

The falor slowed down the reindeers by a group of trees. From there they had a good view over the mountain and shelter at the same time. Elle and Moltas quickly built a windbreak, Nol and Sira fed the reindeers and Interpreter checked that the instructions were in a safe place. Mother and Father gnome placed the little gnomes between themselves under the windbreak and together with the other they formed a circle. The peregrines kept watch outside.

Mother gnome took up her famous bread and Father gnome poured ancient water in small cups. Sira felt her stomach rumbling.

"I wonder where Skade is. We should have seen her a long time ago," whispered one fala.

"Yes, it's really strange. Where can she be?" said the other and took some bread.

"She will surely come. Now we have to put our plan in motion. Does everybody know what to do?" said Interpreter who thought it was difficult to speak in a low voice. His own importance didn't quite come through in a proper way. Interpreter struck his fur gloved hand across the medal on his chest and took a deep breath:

"Well now, it is time. Falor, first you have to get past the big Vitorm which is coiled around the foot of the mountain. The entrance is probably on the front side of the mountain, somewhere close to Vitorm's head. Remember that its eyes are always open but if the spinous mane along its head is down then it's asleep. That is when you have your chance. To find the entrance you will probably need to shape-shift both once and twice and maybe even three times. Can you do that in such a short time?"

The falor glanced at each other and nodded.

"We'll make it." Their eyes shifted in orange and yellow and soon they were gone.

"I really wonder how they do that? Disappear before you even wink. And did you see their eyes?" Elle looked at the others and rolled her own eyes.

"Elle! That you will never know. Now focus. If we do not manage to kill Vitorm, we are dead," said Interpreter and his gaze made Elle stiffen.

"Tell me about Vitorm and what you and Moltas are going to do so I know that you have understood," urged Interpreter.

He drank some of the ancient water and Elle looked at Moltas.

"Vitorm is very dangerous and guards the Black Mountain for Elakka, so no one can enter. It's also very long and it's coiled up around the foot of the mountain.

It's very good at camouflaging itself, so it's important to look out and not come too close or touch it. Because then it can turn even meaner than it is and inject poison into your body or even use its huge fangs on you…" said Elle and got such cold creeps that she had to interrupt herself. She looked at Moltas again and continued:

"You've to use a special way to kill it. Moltas and I are going to make three fires and then Vitorm will slither through the fires. And then, when it's slithered through the third fire, it'll turn into ashes," said Elle and Sira took her hand.

"Good Elle! You remember everything. We can do this," said Sira and tried to sound calm.

"Very good. A couple of lantern carriers will accompany you so that you can find wood for the fires," said Interpreter.

"Remember to light all three fires, one by one."

Interpreter turned to Nol.

"It's only you who can talk to the animals. And you are very brave to dare to trick Vitorm to slither through the fires."

Nol was proud of himself. He thought about the secret which the lynx had whispered in his ear. Suddenly, one of the falor was back.

"We've found Skade! She's been frozen and lies not far from the foot of the mountain to the left. We heard pecking and gurgling sounds and saw that some ravens were trying to get to her," said fala with a dark voice.

"Is she dead?" asked Interpreter.

"No, she's alive but refrigerated and I think it'll take many hours for her to melt. We must get Elakka first. Vitorm woke up just when we arrived and it won't sleep for another while," said fala and straightened her cap.

"No one has caught sight of you yet?" Interpreter continued.

"I don't think so. But Vitorm seems to have a strong sense of smell, so we've to be extra careful so it doesn't trace us. I've to hurry back. Start the fires as soon as possible," said fala authoritatively.

"We'll take care of it at once," answered Moltas and saluted. He and Elle stood up and left.

Interpreter took out a napkin and dried his forehead.

"Oh dear, oh dear. I hope everything will go without a hitch. Mother and Father gnome, when the falor have found the entrance it is your turn. Are you prepared?" he urged.

"Yes," they said in one voice and picked up the little gnomes in their arms.

"There are a couple of bushes quite close to the front side of the mountain. Tiptoe over there and wait for the falor's signal. The peregrines will show you the way", said Interpreter and looked around.

"What's Elakka done?" Sira asked Interpreter. "Why was she fettered inside a mountain? Why does she have to be destroyed? What have I got to do with all this?"

Sira felt that she had to have answers to the questions she'd had for so long but Interpreter shook his head and worriedly said to her:

"I might not have answers to all your questions right now but I can say as much that Elakka and the Queen were the best of sisters a long time ago. But then something happened, which I do not have time to tell you now, and Elakka cut the ties with the Queen with the help of a spell. In the end, it affected you humans, so badly that your children were born without imagination in their souls. And there are only a few of the elderly who can use their imagination and pass on the stories. One of them is your grandmother."

Sira met Interpreter's urging gaze.

"Now hurry, Sira. You know what to do. It is time," called Interpreter.

Sira hardly understood half of what Interpreter had told her but somewhere deep inside she felt the anger towards Elakka grow. Elakka wouldn't win, she thought while she sneaked out of the windbreak. A peregrine landed on her shoulder to be her eyes in the dark.

Vitorm

Nol stood only a few metres from Vitorm. He felt like Boreal's smallest gnome when he looked up at the dirty white body of the snake. Vitorm's head swayed backwards and forwards and the big eyes were spying and searching. The thorny grey-white mane stood straight up.

When it breathed, the nostrils became big dark holes and out of its mouth came the most repulsive stench you could think of. Nol's body shivered and felt how fear wanted to drag him away. But he managed to get hold of himself and took a few steps closer.

Vitorm opened its mouth and a forked tongue shot out between the monstrous fangs. Nol was happy that it hadn't noticed him yet. He gathered courage and sneaked right below the snake's head and whispered:

"Psst."

The snake took no notice.

"Psst. Hello!"

Still no reaction. Nol couldn't see any ear. *Maybe it's hard of hearing,* Not thought and tried to raise his voice:

"Hello there, Vitorm! Can you hear me? Hello?" Nol jumped up and down. He noticed that the first fire was lit a bit further away. "Hello! Hello! Vitorm, my name's Nol and I must speak with you."

The snake's body stiffened and the giant head turned quickly towards him. Nol thought that he would be snake food before he realised that he was looking straight into one of Vitorm's big eyes.

"Who's disturbing me?" Vitorm had no voice. It was as if it spoke inside Nol's head.

"It's me, Nol. I didn't mean to disturb you but I've a proposal for you."

Nol was startled when Vitorm's eye came closer.

"A proposal? Are you bothering me with a proposal?" snorted Vitorm. Its breath made Nol feel sick. He saw that the other fire was lit as well.

"Yes, I've heard from a reliable source that you're afraid of fire. And I know that there are many laughing at you for it." Nol felt a bit more secure and straightened himself up.

"What? Are they laughing at me? At *me*? Be careful not to tell lies." Vitorm's voice roared inside Nol's head.

"It's true. There are many laughing at you and say that you're a cowardly snake. But I can help you prove them wrong," said Nol in a loud voice.

"Me? A cowardly snake? I'm the king of snakes. That's impudent! And how exactly could a little thing like yourself help me with such a big thing?" roared Vitorm with its eye staring straight at him.

The third fire was lit and Nol saw his chance.

"If you look over there, you will see there are three fires burning. If you can slither through those three fires I promise I'd tell everybody that you're brave and strong and not at all afraid of fires. Then everybody will fear you again."

Vitorm gazed at the fires and Nol heard inside his head:

"It's a trifle. To slither through three fires is nothing for someone like me." It bit its tail and rolled towards the fires.

"It's coming this way! Elle! Quickly!" Moltas grabbed Elle's arm when he saw Vitorm approaching. He dragged her behind a big snowdrift. It hissed and sizzled when Vitorm gallantly slithered through the first fire.

"Ugh, what a smell! I feel sick," said Elle and covered her nose and mouth with her mitten. Moltas peeked from behind the snow pile.

"It's going for the second now." Moltas held his breath.

"I can't watch," said Elle with her mitten still over her nose and mouth.

Despite Vitorm's skin being a little burnt, it managed to slither through the second fire. When it slithered through the third fire its skin started to burn and its meat to fry.

Vitorm's frightful howling echoed far away in the mountaintops. And then it almost slithered out of the fire but then remembered that everybody would think that he was a coward and laugh at him if he did. Shame on him for giving up.

Vitorm used its last strength to get through the fire. Just when it thought that it had completed its mission, its body slowly turned into ashes. Nol rushed to Elle and Moltas.

"Well done! It was more gullible than I thought," whispered Nol. Moltas put his arm around Elle and smiled through his beard.

"It was really scary. But I managed to save some of Vitorm's meat to make a soup of. I've heard it's good for you," said Elle and held up the grey-white meat and the others made faces.

"Go back to the windbreak now. Hurry!" hissed Nol.

"But you're coming as well, aren't you?" Moltas took hold of Nol's arm.

"No, I've one more thing to do. It's a secret. Not even Interpreter knows about it. Hurry up now!" answered Nol.

The entrance

It was easier for the falor to find the entrance when Vitorm was reduced to ashes. They searched backwards and forwards, up and down along the brownish side of the mountain. They used the eyes of the falcon and the climbing skills of the squirrel. Their invisible hands wandered across the uneven and sharp surface. In some places the water ran down and the smell was stale. In other places ice was glued to the side and they shape-shifted into woodpeckers and pecked the ice into bits with their beaks.

Finally, they found it, the entrance. The falor groped about for their bags on their belts and threw the contents at the gate and at the same time quietly repeated a rhyme:

Ye old entrance in the mountain wall
Hidden here behind it all
Open up your secret door
And change will be for ever more.

The gate opened sideways and they looked into darkness. The falor waved to Mother and Father gnome who rushed forward with the little gnomes in their arms and that was lucky because out of the darkness inside the mountain flew mylingar on ravens. They shouted and roared and waved with their spears.

Mother and Father gnome threw up the little gnomes one by one towards the flying mylingar even though they were afraid that the spears would hit the little gnomes which would then die of poisoning. The ravens' warty beaks grumbled and clicked after them as they came up in the air. But as soon as a little gnome landed on a raven's back, it jumped on a myling's shoulder, grabbed its tangled hair, leant against its ear and said:

"I give you my name. My name is…"

When a myling got the little gnome's name it went up in smoke and the raven changed into a ptarmigan which, with a growling, snoring sound, flew the little gnome to the windbreak where Interpreter, Moltas and Elle waited for them. The lantern carriers used their weak light so that all of them were found.

"What awful creatures. You were so good," said Elle and lifted some of them up in her arms.

"They're so high-pitched and violent. They really shouldn't be allowed to carry spears. And especially not poisonous ones. Luckily, it's all over," said Moltas and wiped his forehead.

"Neither should they be at large. But now Elakka's spies have gone up in smoke and the ravens are gone. Little gnomes, you're a credit to Boreal," said Interpreter and gave them each a piece of a spruce shoot which they happily munched on.

"How could mylingar go up in smoke just like that?" asked Elle.

"Inquisitive Elle," said Interpreter and shook his head. "They didn't just 'go up in smoke'. Mylingar are the nameless children who have lost their imagination and they fly around looking for their name. But then Elakka must have got hold of them and made them her spies. The trick was to let the little gnomes give mylingar their names and then they didn't have to look for it any more and went up in smoke." Interpreter straightened his fur cap.

"But what about the ravens? How could they change into ptarmigans?" continued Elle.

"Do not ask any more questions. You need to rest now. Where is Nol by the way? He should also be here."

Interpreter looked around and Elle and Moltas glanced at each other.

"He stayed on," said Moltas finally. "He said that he had something secret to do."

"Something secret? What kind of secret thing? He cannot do anything that is not in the instructions!" Interpreter unfolded the leather document.

"I cannot see anything about a secret thing here. It is better I go…" He read the document again. "No, I cannot. My task is to stay here with you. We can only hope that the secret thing does not spoil anything."

Interpreter folded the leather document and the other hand stroked nervously across the medal on his chest.

Inside the Black Mountain

When the falor, Nol, Mother and Father gnome stepped inside the dark mountain, an ice-cold chilliness grabbed them and a horrible stench met them. They knew they could easily get lost in the passages but they didn't dare to have any light to guide them. They had to fumble along the rugged walls dripping of damp and old vegetation.

The bumpy and partly swampy ground made them trip over several times. And the further they got inside the mountain's narrow passage the colder it got.

"Ugh! It's so cold." The icicles in Father gnome's beard clung weakly when he spoke.

"I'm freezing," said Nol and Mother gnome lifted him up in her arms to warm him a little.

"Shh! Don't talk. You can't even whisper," said the fala at the front and stopped.

The passage split in two and the fala hesitated. Then a strong cold chill pushed them to the right. They could do nothing but continue forward. The rugged walls soon became smooth and slimy and it was harder to keep their balance when their hands couldn't get a grip on anything. And the now dry and decayed ground made every step echo in the walls. Suddenly, a voice cracked like rockets between the walls.

"Hahaha! I knew you were coming. I've my spies. Hahaha! Come in, come in. Enter my palace." The voice was sharp and a light drew their steps towards it.

"I know who you are," said the voice again. "It must be my sister who's sent you. Come on in. Come in," the voice chuckled.

They stood in the opening of a well-lit large cave deep inside the mountain. The rotten smell from the passage was even stronger here. There was dirt and filth everywhere and smoke came from pots and pans. Old broken cobwebs with dead insects hung from the ceiling. Skeleton parts dangled from a stretched rope and struck a muffled steady sound when they bumped into each other. Mother gnome shivered at the thought of where the skeleton parts could have come from.

It crept and crawled on the walls which trickled with damp and the floor was muddy.

"Don't just stand there. Enter!" the sharp voice shouted.

Something or someone pushed them inside. Father gnome thought that he could never use his slippers again after this horrifying visit.

They entered the cave. And there stood Elakka. She was disgracefully changed. The bleak, sunken face was barely visible behind the long, tangled dark-green hair. Her evil eyes stared and between the dry black lips were yellow-stained teeth. Her nose was sharp as the beak of an eagle. Her body was skinny after all the years in imprisonment and the too-big black dress was held together by a belt. Nol saw to his great horror that the belt contained a big knife and dead rats and birds were strung it. Around her neck and arms snakes in gold and silver wriggled. With bony hands, crooked fingers and nails sharp as claws, she stood stirring a big pot.

"I know that my sister, who calls herself Queen, can't come by herself. That's why you're here, Father and Mother gnome, protectors," she grunted.

They looked at each other. Elakka didn't mention Nol's name. Hadn't she seen him? Quickly, the falor pushed Nol behind them.

"She thinks that you can destroy me and bring imagination back. That's where she's wrong. You can't do anything about it. I'll never reveal the spell. I'm glad I cut the ties. That it's *me* and *only* me who owns imagination. Hahaha!"

Elakka took one of the dead rats from her belt and threw it in the pot. It sizzled and a greenish acid reek went up to the ceiling. She continued stirring the pot and said in a hoarse voice:

"Soon I'll put you in the pot as well. It'll be a true pleasure to cook you slowly. Hahaha! Hahaha!"

Elakka's vicious laughter never seemed to end and the falor saw their chance. Nol hid behind a big pot and the falor shape-shifted. They dashed towards Elakka and climbed up along her back and hung from and clung to her tangled hair. Elakka hit and waved her bony arms, trying to catch them with her crooked fingers.

"What are these rats clinging to my hair? I thought I'd killed all the horrible creatures. Just you wait, I'll get you and throw you in the pot, you rubbish!" she roared.

The rats were fast and swung in her hair as if it were lianas. She put her arms behind her back as far as she could and her crooked fingers fumbled up and down.

Mother and Father gnome ran towards a big stone on the other side of the cave. They pushed away the stone, ran into a small passage behind it and entered a small cavity. Fire torches on the wall lit up the treasures spread out all over the ground: gold, silver, diamonds and sapphires; everything you could wish for. Mother gnome bent down and picked up a necklace of the purest gold. A rustling sound came from one of the corners and soon the necklace turned into gravel.

She looked surprised at Father gnome who held a stone in his hand.

"This stone was a diamond just now." Father gnome looked very thoughtful. Quiet giggles were heard and at that moment Mother gnome knew what had happened. "What in all ices' times are *you* doing here?"

Eight wrinkled and dusty faces with green cocked hats on the heads popped up from behind a chest.

"The leprechauns!" Father gnome opened his mouth in astonishment.

The leprechauns stepped forward quite ashamed. Their hands were soiled and sore and their trousers full of holes after carrying and dragging treasures through the narrow passage to the Miner's wife.

"How did you get here? Or rather, how have you dared coming here? To Elakka's Black Mountain? Are you stealing her treasures? Don't you have any sense at all?" said Mother gnome who simply couldn't believe her eyes.

The leprechauns glanced at each other. Elakka's mountain? Was that where they were?

"I don't know what to do with you. And what will the Queen say? She sent you home from the castle, not on any adventures. Stay where you are and don't move. Father gnome and I must find our friend who disappeared from the castle in a black hole. Have you seen a black hole anywhere? With a gnome inside?" she said and gave the leprechauns a fierce look.

The leprechauns shook their heads and sat down. They were quite relieved and thought that they might be saved now and wouldn't have to carry all those treasures to the horrible Miner's wife. She would probably have eaten them afterwards even if they'd behaved themselves.

A soft ringing sound was heard.

"Hello, hello?" It sounded like it came from a voice which bounced far away in one of the passages.

"Did you hear that?" said Father gnome and put his hand behind his ear.

"No, I didn't hear anything. Keep looking," answered Mother gnome and peeked in a chest.

"Hello! Can you hear me? Hello?" said the little voice again.

"Now I hear it. Where does it come from?" said Mother gnome.

"I'm up here. Look up," the voice begged.

Mother and Father gnome looked up. Above them, in a little cage of iron, sat the gnome Bol with his cap askew. He waved.

"There you are, our dear Bol. We've missed you so much," said Mother gnome and clapped her hands.

"How did you get there? We must help you down immediately!" said Father gnome and placed himself underneath the cage.

"How do we do this?" said Father gnome and scratched his beard.

"Please help me down. Hurry up before Elakka comes," urged Bol and jumped around in the cage which made it rock to and fro.

Mother and Father gnome looked helplessly at each other but the leprechauns knew what to do. They dashed forward and placed themselves underneath the cage. Then they climbed up on each other's shoulders and opened the cage door. The gnome jumped out and landed in a pile of silver.

"We must get out of here quickly before Elakka catches sight of us."

The leprechauns dragged the gnomes along, pointing towards the passage they'd come in through.

The bear

Elakka shouted and roared at the rats which ran round and round and drove her mad. Finally, she dropped down and the falor quickly shape-shifted from rats to wolves with piercing teeth. They moved towards her and growled deeply:

"Where's the spell, Elakka?"

"Give us the spell before we turn you into rags!"

Within seconds Elakka shape-shifted to a bear and bawled with big jaws: "You'll never get it!" The bear's paw struck the wolves. Pots and pans flew in every direction. One of the wolves hit the wall and stayed down.

"Imagination will die and that's forever!" The bear caught the other wolf and held it down with its paws. Just when its jaws would slash the wolf in the neck a voice spoke behind one of the pots:

Blueberries, crowberries
Cranberries and lingonberries
In piles outside the mountain gate
Hurry, hurry, hurry
Do not be late.

The bear rose on two legs, opened its jaws and roared all the way up to the mountaintop. Then it turned sharply and disappeared.

It was like the whole place held its breath and when the bear didn't return everything and everybody sighed in relief. Nol crept out of his hideaway behind the pot and the falor shape-shifted again. But the fala, who had been thrown into the wall, lay still and quiet. Nol and the other fala rushed to her. Her eyes were closed, cheeks pale and she bled from a wound in her forehead.

"She's hardly breathing," said the fala and looked around. "Get the mortar over there, Nol. Hurry!"

When Nol came back with the mortar, the fala had loosened the bags from her belt and poured everything into the mortar.

"It's all or nothing. An angry bear claw can do a lot of damage." When the fala had crushed and mixed the contents she took a pinch, put in the wound on the forehead and pressed. She poured out the rest in her hand and blew it over the wounded fala.

"All we can do now is wait and hope for the best. Go and see if you can find Mother and Father gnome. Hopefully, they've found their friend in the black hole. I'm staying here."

Nol zigzagged between pots and pans and other rubbish to the opening where Mother and Father gnome had entered. But all he saw was a lot of treasures. Gold, silver and diamonds. How rich his parents would be if he only took a little.

"Nol! Nol! Did you find them? I think she's waking up now," called the fala.

"I'm coming. There's nobody there. Just a lot of gold and diamonds," answered Nol. The wounded fala sat up and touched her forehead.

"What happened? How's Sira doing? Did she make it?" asked.

"We don't know. We hope. Can you stand up? Nol, did you just say that you didn't find Mother and Father gnome?" asked the other fala.

"Yes, they weren't there. Maybe Elakka's put a spell on them," replied Nol with a tear in his eye.

"And how did you know which rhyme you should use to lure out the bear? I mean to lure out Elakka?" asked the other fala with curiosity.

"A lynx whispered it to me," said Nol and straightened himself up.

"A lynx? A lynx and you, Nol, saved us. Now we've got to get out of here. Sira might need our help. We can look for the gnomes later."

The reckoning

Sira was well hidden outside the mountain door and waited. Interpreter had said that Elakka probably would shape-shift and Sira must attack whatever came out from the door no matter what it was. And Sira was prepared to the teeth.

This was the most important task she'd had in her whole life and she wouldn't fail. She thought about her mum and nan. She missed them. She wanted to be with them. She wanted to go home and lie on the blue couch and listen to Nan's stories together with her mum. She wanted her mum to stop working and become herself again. She wanted imagination to come back to humans.

Sira felt like crying and did everything she could to gulp down her tears. She must pull herself together, she thought and wiped her face with one hand. She must be on her guard.

A roar came from inside the mountain and a large bear came rushing out straight towards Sira's hiding place. Its jaws struck and its eyes rolled. The peregrine cried and flew up above the bear. Had it caught sight of her already? It rose on two legs and fought with its paws. Its jaws drooled. Sira plucked up courage, stood up and shouted:

"Would you like some nice berries?" She cupped her hands. The bear got down on all fours and sniffed the air.

"If you want my nice berries I want something from you," she said. The bear looked bewildered.

"If you want my nice berries I want the spell. The spell which mends the bond between the Queen and Elakka. The bond that gives imagination and stories life again," said Sira self-assuredly.

The bear flew into a temper and stared at her with ominous eyes.

"Give me the spell and you'll get the berries." Sira reached out her hands. She didn't have any berries but it was the best she could think of.

The bear opened its jaws and roared.

"I'm not afraid of you!" shouted Sira and fixed her eyes on the bear. She hoped she wouldn't be eaten. She took out some silver bullets from her pocket.

"If you don't give me the spell you'll get these in you," she said and showed her hand to the bear. The silver bullets shone like stars.

"Silver bullets kill a bear but not me. Hahaha!"

And the bear, which was prepared to attack, shapeshifted.

Elakka stood right in front of her. She was one of the most horrific creatures Sira had ever seen. But she pulled herself together and shouted:

"I'll give you one more chance. Give me the spell!"

"Hahaha! Never! Imagination shall die!" screamed Elakka and took out a small box. "I've the spell here for safekeeping. Hahaha!"

She held up the box and in the middle of her most terrible laugh, the box fell out of her hands. With the speed of lightning, one of the falor swept by, snatched the box and threw it to Sira.

"Here Sira! Catch!

Sira caught the box and opened it faster than... Quickly she read the rhyme, once forward and twice backwards.

I hereby cut the bond
And take all imagination
Both from Boreal
And the humans
Imagination shall disappear forever
And nothing will remain

Elakka turned into stone. When Sira read the rhyme backwards a second time, Elakka fell into pieces and disappeared into the ground. The only things left were her torn black dress and some bones.

Epilogue

Sira woke with a start and looked around drowsily. She was lying on her grandmother's blue couch. Her grandmother sat in the armchair with a cup of coffee in her hands.

"Is it time to wake up now, Sira?" chuckled grandmother.

Sira rubbed her eyes. "Are you okay now, Nan?"

"Okay?" asked grandmother and looked at Sira over the rim of her glasses.

"Yes, I managed to break the spell between the Queen and Elakka so imagination could return," said Sira and sat herself up. She was still a bit drowsy.

"Lucky for me that you succeeded with your task," smiled grandmother secretively.

The doorbell rang and her mother came in.

"I can see you're having a cosy time," said mother. She sat down next to Sira and gave her a warm hug. "I guess your nan's told you one of her fantastic stories again," she continued and smiled at grandmother, who took a sip of her coffee.

Sira looked in surprise at her grandmother and started laughing out loud.

She said: "It's so typical of you, Nana! You always make me believe that your stories are for real!"

Grandmother's wrinkled face smiled at her and she put her cup down on the table as she said:

"Imagination is wonderful, isn't it? I'm so glad you like listening to my stories, Sira."

Her mother cleared her throat and said:

"You know what? I'm not going to have two jobs any more. I'll only work during the day from now on. I got a raise today and that money will be enough for us, Sira."

"Yippee!" shouted Sira. She could barely believe it was true. She threw herself off the couch and danced around in the living room.

Mother and grandmother laughed.

"It's good news," said grandmother. Then you'll have more time for us," grandmother winked at Sira.

"And that's not all. Look what I've bought for you, Sira," said mother and took out a parcel.

Sira dashed to her mother and gave her a hug. "Wow, can I open it now?"

"Of course," answered her mother happily. "I hope you're going to like it."

Sira hurried to open it. In the parcel were a sketchbook, a package of brushes and best of all, new acrylic colours. Sira first looked at her mother and then her grandmother and exclaimed, "Thanks a million, Mum! They're really nice!"

She hugged her mother and then her grandmother. When she opened the sketchbook, a small feather from an eagle was on the first page.

"Now I'm going to paint!" she shouted. "I'm going to paint the Queen and Elakka. And all of Boreal!"

It was the crack of dawn when Sira rode the bike home from grandmother's house. She knew exactly which picture she was going to paint first. When she approached the front of the house, she saw two grey-clad characters standing on the porch. They took off their grey caps and bowed to her. Sira laughed and had just time to wave to them before they disappeared somewhere underneath the house.